ALSO BY LEA CARPENTER

red white blue
Eleven Days

Ilium

Ilium

LEA CARPENTER

Alfred A. Knopf

NEW YORK 2024

THIS IS A BORZOI BOOK
PUBLISHED BY ALFRED A. KNOPF

Copyright © 2024 by Lea Carpenter

www.aaknopf.com

Knopf, Borzoi Books, and the colophon are registered
trademarks of Penguin Random House LLC.

Library of Congress Cataloging-in-Publication Data
Names: Carpenter, Lea, author.
Title: Ilium / Lea Carpenter.
Description: First edition. | New York : Alfred A. Knopf, 2024.
Identifiers: LCCN 2023002574 (print) | LCCN 2023002575 (ebook) |
ISBN 9780593536605 (hardcover) | ISBN 9780593536612 (ebook)
Subjects: LCGFT: Thrillers (Fiction) | Spy fiction. | Novels.
Classification: LCC PS3603.A7698 I55 2024 (print) | LCC PS3603.A7698
(ebook) | DDC 813/.6—dc23/eng/20230123
LC record available at https://lccn.loc.gov/2023002574
LC ebook record available at https://lccn.loc.gov/2023002575

Jacket images: (figure) msan10/Getty Images: (background)
Sergey Ryumin/Getty Images
Jacket design by Janet Hansen

Manufactured in the United States of America
First Edition

For my mother,
Carroll,
Who gave me a love for stories

Then the new style began.

—John le Carré

Contents

I LONDON *1*

II GARDEN *7*

III LOBSTERS *25*

IV ARCACHON *47*

V KING OF KINGS *67*

VI JACK AND JILL *81*

VII A COMPLICATED MAN *101*

VIII WHAT IS DONE
CANNOT BE UNDONE *137*

IX ILIUM *171*

X SUGAR CUBES *201*

XI BEIRUT *215*

I

LONDON

Could she feel them?

The two sets of eyes on her, that day in Trafalgar Square, one belonging to a young man on a skateboard, the other to an artist painting watercolors by the statue of King George IV. Or were there more than two sets, maybe there were four, maybe more. How many people were watching her that day and what were they looking for, or, guarding her against. And was it only men or was there a woman watching, too, usually there is a woman as women are less likely to elicit suspicion. What did they see in her. Whatever it was, it was something she had failed to see in herself, some singular mark of significance, something that made her uniquely valuable. And so, as she boarded that bus in Central London that day, the same bus she boarded every even slightly rainy day at that time in her life, she had no idea she was being watched. The only thing on her mind was hunger, and she was chastising herself for skipping breakfast then wasting time at work, as a result of which she was, at that moment, late to lunch. She was asking herself if she was the only person in the world who ate alone most days and when and if that would change. She was running casually through a familiar list of things she knew she could improve in her life.

At the top of that list was, *be less boring*, followed closely by, *take new risks*. She boarded the bus and, as always, took any window seat she could find, preferably at the back, where no one would bother her. She was a creature of habit, part of the problem with that list. As the bus pulled into traffic, she looked back and could see a small crowd gathering on the steps of the National Gallery, reminding her of another thing she was missing. She added to the list, *learn more about the world*.

If she had looked a little more closely, she might have noticed a man standing slightly apart from the crowd, just below the entrance to the museum. The museum was opening late that day to launch a new exhibit of old master drawings. If she had looked a little more closely the man on the stairs would have stood out to her not because he was wearing dark glasses even in the light rain. Or because he was wearing an ill-fitting sweater with the Manchester United logo, the one with a devil in the center. She would have noticed him because he was handsome, and she was young and single then, and not happy about the latter. It would not have occurred to her that those glasses and that sweater were selected explicitly to distract you from the man's looks. He was handsome in a way it was hard not to notice. His looks were an inconvenience.

He had arrived in London early that morning from Paris. On his flight, he had read all about the young woman, though there was not much to read. He had learned why she had been chosen, and though he would ultimately be the one to approve this operation and her role in it, he always had doubts, starting out, about new recruits. Especially for a case like this. It was his nature to anticipate catastrophe, to believe no one is who they seem to be. And it was his absolute conviction that the perfectly innocent asset did not exist, innocence being a chimera, in his world. You see, the man on the steps of the National Gallery that rainy morning in Central London had grown up in a world far away from the world of the young woman on the bus, in a country defined not by its long-lost empire or its football stars, by Shakespeare or Churchill or errant princes, but rather by poverty, civil wars, a rich history of loss. His world had hardened him early on and formed the essence of what made him excel at his job. His job was, above all, making wise assessments about people. His job was seducing you into risk. "Life and death work, this," one of his colleagues put it once, joking not joking. Though the truth is, a lot of espionage is simply watching and waiting—speaking of *be less boring*. A lot of espionage is marking time, holding out for a reckoning that just might save a life. Some spies he knew referred to their profession, as, simply, babysitting.

"People are children and children are fickle and cruel," was what his first boss had said. His first boss, who had no children, who taught him the First Rule of spy craft was not *do unto others as you would have others do unto you* but rather, *mind your six*. Watch your back. And yet for all his cold-blooded worldview, the man on the stairs of the National Gallery that day watched as the bus picked up speed and as the young woman, seated in the back by a window, traced the outline of a heart on her fog-stained window. From this simple act he drew several conclusions. She was a romantic, a dreamer, an optimist. She was interested in love. She was open to experience.

*

The period right before the recruitment of a new asset is defined by the knowledge you are about to change someone's life. That you will tell every lie you need to tell to do it. You will manipulate, control, abuse, seduce, deny. You will spoil and bribe, you will backflip off any high dive. You will ruthlessly promise her the moon and believe you can deliver it. Above all you will convince her she is operating with free will, she is in control, this is her chance. You will do these things because achieving your goal is far more urgent than any consequences of breaking her heart. And the man on the stairs of the National Gallery that day knew from breaking hearts. And from broken ones.

He had waited a long time to find this young woman, and he did not plan to let her go. He knew that her bus was headed to Oxford Circus, just a short distance away. He knew that there she would eat in the small sandwich shop she liked while reading the *Daily Mail* on her phone. Her need for routine, her taste for gossip, these things were neither novel nor rare, but they indicated an emptiness. And that emptiness was one thing he and his colleagues, one colleague above all, could not have predicted yet from which they would profit. The young woman was not yet trained, or even particularly educated, but she was dissatisfied, the hallmark of vulnerability. And as she traced that heart on the foggy window the man on the stairs removed his glasses. He closed his eyes. If you had been standing near him you might have noticed he seemed emotional and wondered if those were tears, or raindrops, in his eyes. What you could not possibly have known was that those tears were tears of relief. A very long wait was over, its reckoning a bird in his hand. And now something new could be born.

II

GARDEN

There was a private garden near the house where my mother worked, in Central London, as the personal assistant to a wealthy widow. Each day after school I took the Tube, from an area where there were no gardens, to meet her. And each day, on the walk from the Tube to the white Georgian house where the widow lived, I passed by that garden's locked iron gates, accessible only with a key. The keys, my mother explained, were given to only ten lucky families who owned houses nearby. The widow had a set, though she never shared them with my mother. She never thought to offer her employee's young child a chance to play in the garden while waiting for her mother to finish typing up a thank-you note, ordering more fresh raspberries, making a bed. "Assistant" was a euphemism for housekeeper. "Assistant" gave my mother a professional gloss she liked and took pride in. "Assistant" was the word she used and had chosen for herself. I never knew what my mother did in that house until many years later. I never would have imagined how much she hated it or that she was always tired and that, when I once asked why she was tired she said she was tired "of pretending." I didn't understand that at all. To pretend is to escape yourself, and at one time, escape was all I wanted. Pretend I am a princess trapped in a castle with crenellated walls. Pretend I am Joan of Arc, Queen Elizabeth, an Olympic archer. Pretend I am happy. The line between what it meant to pretend and what it meant to lie, if there was one, didn't concern me then. Then, I was sure if only I could enter that garden, I could be anyone I wanted to be. *Pretending*, I can hear my very young self say in response to my mother, *is not tiring. Pretending is freedom.*

The idea of a private garden was foreign to me and yet at the same time weirdly seductive. It implied an invisible hierarchy and the idea that there are things to which you can, or should, aspire. It implied ideas about ownership and access and privacy, an elite, and everything that I was not part of, despite my mother's fantasies and pretensions. The locked garden implied I was outside of something. My mother was generous with us though we had very little. There were new shoes at the start of school, presents under the tree. But there was also always a sense of living on the edge, the specter that this might be the last pair of shoes that fit, the last trip to the ice rink. The last luxury. And when that happened, I was ready. I had learned to rely almost entirely on my imagination, which was active, for entertainment and pleasure. I would tell myself stories on those Tube rides, and those walks, and central to those stories was that garden. Imagining what was inside, imagining the existence of a gardener who, in my version, possessed magic powers, like an ability to make a rose immortal. I told myself the gardener had inherited his job from his father, and his father before him, that his entire life was the garden, and that he had his own home near the far gate where he would sit on occasion with the owners of those keys and hear their stories, a priest receiving confession. I imagined the lives of the key holders and how they had come to live in this part of the world, this part of London that felt out of a fairy tale. I believed they must have each chosen this spot because of the garden. That garden. It was how I forced order onto what was otherwise a very tumultuous situation, my childhood. I wanted to do everything right, then, and so all the repressed desire for rebellion went into my stories. Even now, I can recall easily each detail of my conjured world. Even now, I keep roses on my desk the color of the roses that peeked through the gates.

I tracked time, then, by which flowers came into bloom throughout the year. Those gates had set my mind on never wanting to be on the outside of anything. What the garden taught me was that the allocation of keys in life isn't fair, that luck and happiness are not prone to reason or will. Unlike a garden, something I assumed was maintained by care and investment, life for me at that time was an experience of chaos. I can see myself at six standing at those gates. And I remember, as clearly as if it had happened an hour ago, the first time I saw someone inside. It was not a unicorn, or some other mythical beast. It was not the gardener, though I did eventually meet the man who tended the garden, and he shared stories with me of all of the key holders, and of course they were nothing like the characters I had imagined. It would turn out that most of them rarely used the garden at all. No, the first person I saw inside those gates was a little girl. She was about my age. It was raining that day and she was wearing a white dress, an act of confidence in a muddy garden. As if she didn't care what might happen. As if she didn't need to care. It occurred to me that she probably had people who took care of her, like most children. No one had ever taken care of me. Only later would I understand the upside of that.

Fifteen years later, and ensconced unhappily in my first job, I was invited to a party at one of the houses that bordered the garden. The wealthy widow had died when I was a teenager and I hadn't been back to those gates, to that area, in ages. Going back might mean admitting my life wasn't moving in the right direction, that things were *not* getting better, or easier, that I wasn't accruing anything, except debt. By my late teens and as my parents slowly tore themselves apart with anger and arguments, I was swapping out boyfriends and placing pins in maps of places I wanted to go one day, New Caledonia, Cappadocia, Saint Petersburg. One day, I told myself, I would exit my family's long-standing tradition of resistance to progress. I would leave behind their gray lives and enter a world of color, romance. I had not yet become the woman I knew I was meant to be. The cliff jumper. The free climber. The key holder. That woman wouldn't look longingly at maps. She would take risks.

At the party that night near the garden I remember looking at all the other guests, certain I was going to run into that little girl I had seen through the gates. I believed that, when we finally met, we would realize that while all I had ever wanted was to get inside the garden, all that she had ever wanted was to get out. You see, I was starting to develop a level of emotional intelligence even if I failed to understand how to use it. I didn't meet her, but it was at that party I learned that the garden was no longer run according to the system of keys and joint ownership but rather had been purchased by an entrepreneur. "At what price," I had asked, and the response was, "You can't imagine." I learned that the new owner didn't like roses or really any flowers at all, that he had chosen to gut the garden and to re-create an immaculate Japanese meditation space, complete with twin koi ponds and a Zendo, a space defined by almost invisible rows of symmetrically placed sandstone paths inlaid with circles of sand-colored gravel one could navigate while, ideally, having deep thoughts about the universe. In the place of a pair of antique Persian iron chairs, the new owner had installed a modernist steel bench designed by some celebrated artist I had never heard of to inspire, I gathered, the cleanest possible contemplation of nirvana.

I would learn a lot about the origins of those gravel paths when, at another party four weeks later, the very proud owner of the garden, thirty-three years my senior with a casual charisma as he moved through the room, walked right into my life.

The interesting thing is, by the time I had said yes to his proposal of marriage—it didn't take long—and absorbed the idea that I was going to be the owner of the thing that had symbolized so much to me for so long, it didn't seem absurd at all. It didn't even seem a coincidence, or something you encounter in a fairy tale or myth and know you're meant not to mock as unreal. What it *did* feel like was something I had longed for but never been able to articulate. A path. A triumph over my short history of disarray, and trauma. It actually felt, above all, like the end of something. Though of course it was just another beginning.

His name was Marcus.

"Like Aurelius," he said, on introducing himself. He had little lines like that for everything. Marcus was American, which felt exotic.

People think girls marry much older men as a result of having lost their fathers too young, but the allure for me was less the specter of replacement paternal protection than the idea that Marcus needed me, too. He needed me more than I needed him. Later I would look back and see that in his mind Marcus's singular accomplishment was deciding to commit to me. He had been, he told me, a career bachelor, devoted to the practice of, in his words, "recreational intimacy." Before meeting me, apparently, Marcus's view of women assured him they all had one thing in common—they would all be happier for having been, if only briefly, colonized by him. And his world.

And it was a world, with Marcus. You didn't just hook up with him, you hooked up with the experiences that pleased him and the places he enjoyed, owned, or felt comfortable in. The culture was only entering a period, then, in which rootlessness was in vogue, and Marcus was an early adopter of the idea that you can live everywhere and nowhere, an idea defined by the absence of family. Family means children, roots. Family means consistency and routine.

With Marcus there was no routine. Aligning with him was to align with a set of ideas and belief systems, that included a reverence for excess always coupled with regular bouts of outrageous asceticism. The eight-figure purchase of a meditation garden, for example, and the destruction of thousands of rare roses to make way for a prayer bench. Marcus kept a minister on his payroll, though he'd never been to church. The "vicar," as Marcus called him, was from Boston, and he prepared daily lessons and blessings that, according to Marcus, promised "absolution on the margin." Marcus admired belief systems but could never select then settle into just one. On seeing the beach at night in Tel Aviv, he considered converting to Judaism, but later back in Rome he was all about the epic glory of the Vatican, especially how they managed their money, the fact that "they never even pay a fee."

Every woman who ever met Marcus, according to Marcus, had wanted to *know* him. And yet Marcus, I would understand early on, didn't want to be known. I never asked him to confess any sins, and I didn't ask him why he had chosen me, a girl with nothing more than a secondary school education. I was so different from the girls who I would learn had preceded me, girls with Ivy League degrees and club memberships, girls who considered themselves special. Beautiful girls. I had never felt special at all. I had felt, in many ways, like a freak. Sometimes when I looked in the mirror in the early days it occurred to me Marcus had simply chosen me because I was young. Or, like the famous explorer said of Everest, because I was there.

"What do you want for Christmas," he asked, in advance of the first holiday we'd spend together.

"A baby," I said, which was not the planned response.

I was about to turn twenty-one.

"You see that's exactly why I adore you," he said. "You don't fuck around."

Marcus had, he told me, made his fortune "fast, the old-fashioned way," by finding his comparative advantage then working harder than anyone else. And, because he wasn't born into it, he loved spending money, and fiercely demanded a life fully stocked with the results. When we met, he was barely into his fifties and looked barely into his forties. Only the very edge of his appetites had been tempered by time and experience. Some men in their fifties act out in irrational ways in an effort to stall time, and the most popular irrational way is not a sports car but rather to find a woman from another generation to make them feel young. You can't understand this until you're inside the experience of it. I would learn how his childhood had been brutal enough to forgive a lifetime of later indulgence, of choices that appeared vulgar to the casual observer. In the end Marcus indulged less than he encouraged others to do, all at his expense. It was an ability to *host* that thrilled him above all, the ability to crowd every environment he entered with people who kept him from ever having a deep thought, or pain. Ironic, considering his flashy nods to enlightenment. And yet so very Marcus. Marcus gave irony and contradiction a new edge. He reveled in his contradictions. He deplored easily cracked codes. He was, like me, restless. It was the reason he didn't sleep. "Sleep," he would say to anyone who proselytized its merits, "is the only thing that won't go to bed with me."

And so it went that, after that party where we first met, we spent Christmas in the mountains, and then it was May and these outrageously beautiful actors from the Oxford Shakespeare Company were rehearsing *As You Like It* on a sprawling Mallorcan lawn, the kitchens of Marcus's newly acquired "finca" exploding in preparation for our wedding day. Yes, nothing less than a full-blown, highly personalized production of a play by a "a real writer," as Marcus put it, would serve as an appropriate herald of our love, though behind my back others expressed skepticism. His friends, not mine, made up the guest list. I had never had deep friendships, part of my unwillingness to trust. If I had been older, I might have asked some questions. I might have asked, *will a man like Marcus ever really settle down?* Or, *will his energy exhaust me?* Or even, *does money buy happiness and did he just try to buy me?* I organized our story, then, with a selection of relevant facts to suit a certain narrative. At the time, it was the narrative that I was a kind of princess, speaking of fairy tales, that it had simply taken twenty years to meet my prince. The thought was, then, this is all unspooling according to plan.

I had become the little girl in the garden.

I had found myself.

As someone from Marcus's office said casually, "At least he didn't make us sit through *Macbeth*."

Marcus understood limits.

I didn't mind questions around our relationship, the speed of the engagement, how anyone could make that kind of commitment so quickly. I knew what I was doing. At least, I thought I did. To me, marriage was not a life sentence, it was a lifeline. If Marcus was different from anyone in life above all it was from the men who'd defined my childhood. My father and also my drunk uncles, my mother's brothers who only cared for dominating other people because that's what weak men do. Marcus's absolutely apocalyptic desire for life's sensations was one I believed would buoy me out of a learned predisposition toward resistance and cynicism, one that would enable me to change and stop the monologue that had run in loops through my mind forever. Then, I still believed people could change. I believed the experiences of my youth wouldn't mar me for life. I believed Marcus would mellow and that before long we would have dinners for two and spend Sunday mornings reading in bed. What I failed to understand was that Marcus wasn't an ordinary man and his love for me wasn't an ordinary love.

Marcus was a lighthouse.

And lighthouses never switch off. The stakes are too high.

The morning of the wedding Marcus rolled over in bed as sunlight pooled through the windows on three sides and said, "You can still call it off." I think, knowing him, it was more of a flirt than a right hook to my jaw. It may even have been an attempt at empathy, the kind with which Marcus was occasionally able to flip the script on an otherwise consistent sanguinity. I think he woke up, took a look at me, and saw a deer not in headlights, but in the middle of a full-blown crisis, and tried to set the deer free. He looked at me the way a parent looks at a child before that first jab at the doctor's office. A parent wants to take the pain away. I didn't understand that in the moment. In that moment I wanted to find a hammer and smash it through those windows.

Failing to find a hammer I found our wedding cake, sliced a small piece with a very large knife, and brought it all back to

Marcus in bed. I laid the knife on the pillow, and thought about how that cake cost more than the first flat I had lived in. Marcus was on a call with the television running some Spanish soap opera on mute. Marcus was a happy consumer of media, but he seemed to only ever skim the surface of things, claiming to never remember plot or character or meaning. It was part of how he wanted other people to see him, part of his armor of deflection. The truth was that Marcus noticed everything. Marcus could tell you the third line in the fifth scene of the last ten movies he'd watched, the last line of every novel he'd ever read, and the price of the toothpaste today, as adjusted for inflation, he'd used as a child. Marcus was a hawk. And that morning he had looked at that knife on the pillow with admiration, as if my casual act of destruction had pleased him. Most men would consider it insane, a choice like that, but Marcus looked at me that morning like an avid hunter admiring a child who'd just brought home her first kill. Wrecking your wedding cake before the wedding, no one does that, but I did. I didn't realize at the time how much that action told him about me, how it was one more fact in a profile he was rapidly forming. A profile of who I was, who I might become.

"Small," he noted, of the cake, spooling a lick of icing on his finger before slipping it into my mouth.

"Do *you* want to call it off?" I asked.

"I want," he said, pulling on a robe embroidered with Komodo dragons, "to live happily ever after."

He lit a cigarette. Cake, tobacco, not yet nine in the morning. That was Marcus. He would now go spend an hour on the treadmill to repent.

"We are going to define what happiness means, together. No one else matters, not anymore."

And there it was. His interstellar confidence. His clarity that things would work out. His imperviousness to the opinions of others. And the way in which his spoiled-child veneer was always slyly, effectively counterweighted with an inclination toward the philosophical, toward kindness. Sometimes it was easy to forget Marcus was a man who had altered international commodities markets and then, with over half of the proceeds, "given back," always anonymously, always to organizations you've never heard of who participated in things like microloans. "A hundred million dollars can give you a reputation, but a hundred dollars can change your life," he would say, reminding me we had both once been locked outside of something, and would never forget what that felt like.

We went swimming before the ceremony. I remember the simple white dress I wore and the ribbons in my hair and how Marcus wanted an Episcopal service because "it's the shortest." He gave me a simple platinum band with one tiny diamond and when we sat for the Shakespeare, he held my hand and squeezed it three times on hearing the line about "first love." He was the first to stand for an ovation, tears in his eyes. He had listened. He'd been present. And yet within minutes the armor was back on, the mask carefully reaffixed, the Marcus show about to start. As he slipped back into character, I followed his lead.

"You're brave," said a woman who'd arrived that morning from Lisbon and whom Marcus had installed in the house, in the best guest bedroom. Her name was Annabel and she told me she "was a broker," and when I asked what that meant she said, "I move money around." She was maybe ten years older than me. Annabel was Marcus's "very old friend" and, later, Annabel would help me smooth the edges of my ideas of him, who he was, what exactly had happened. Everything about Annabel seemed totally unstudied in a way I envied. And there was never jealousy between us. We both wanted the same thing, it seemed to me. We both wanted Marcus to be happy.

I could tell the first time we met that Annabel didn't suffer fools. Everything about her was impeccable, and my jeans and T-shirts made me feel like her child, in ways, or perhaps I wanted to feel that way, perhaps I was looking not only for a father but for a mother, too. By that time, both my parents were dead. I would be reborn entirely according to Marcus's needs, which sounds simple enough. The problem is, when you reinvent yourself for someone else you are reinventing around your *idea* of what they want, and this will get you into all sorts of trouble. The irony is, a real lover doesn't want you to mirror and please. A real lover wants you independent.

"People think Marcus is a racehorse, but in fact he's a sphinx," she said, watching him move through the crowd at our reception. "And you know, he was in the war." I did know Marcus had served in the military, before going into business; he didn't hide that, nor did he hold it up as something defining. He told me he'd served in Somalia, Libya, and the Middle East, "though not in the trendy spots," and that it was so long ago he had very few memories. Annabel, I would learn, had spent the weeks leading up to the wedding with a Qatari prince whose son had been kidnapped. I had read the story, which didn't mention her name, and when I asked Marcus about it, he told me that "the people who get things done don't get their names in newspapers."

"Why is a broker involved in a kidnapping," I asked, and he'd said, "The answer to that question is currently above my pay grade." I would learn that Annabel had been involved in all kinds of things I would have called dangerous, or even insane. I would learn that Annabel's skill was less with cash and more with information. And people. Marcus teased her about "all her secrets," the gentle mock a cardinal sign of his affection. He teased her as if he himself had no secrets at all. He teased her as if her work was something less than deadly serious.

The wedding night was perfect. All the stars were out, and the actors, having pleased their audience, moved among the guests in costume giving the hilltop the illusion of being an extension of Arden Forest. We had our dance, and Marcus made a speech about true love and how "everything had changed" the moment he saw me. It was romantic and felt true. That night as I got into bed I thought about the garden, and whether I had the courage to ask Marcus to bring back the roses.

Had my entire life and all the other things I had endured been a path to this moment? Somehow it didn't feel quite real yet, like *I* was the actor in a play only the play wasn't Shakespeare. I was making up the lines as I went along. I had no sense of what scene would come next, but as each scene evolved, I could start to see the way I would handle it. It never occurred to me that I wasn't at all in control, that this was *not* the beginning of a new kind of life filled with comfort, the life I had only read about in books. It never occurred to me that the life you have is only in part the life you choose, because the moment you start to think you know what's coming next, that's when lightning strikes, shatters those windows, and rain starts to pool on the floor.

*

We were leaving in an hour for Dubrovnik. Marcus had hired a sailboat to take us up the coast. A small box sat on the sink in our Spanish-tiled bathroom, a tiny card taped on top with my name written in Marcus's taut hand. Inside was a gold key engraved with my initials.

"See Dubrovnik, and Split," Marcus said, explained that was a joke, then admitted he had heard it was Auden's joke, adding "Poets aren't very funny." Marcus had sailed the Dalmatian coast many times and loved teaching me its history. The water in Croatia was a spectacular blue that bled into teal then into an almost fluorescent green as you moved closer to shore. A holiday with Marcus was never absent agenda, and he finally disclosed what his was for this trip at lunch on our second day at sea.

"About the baby," he started.

"What baby," I said.

"Our baby."

He went on to tell me that he wanted to "get pregnant," as if we were doing it together, "immediately," as if pregnancy was as easy as flipping a switch, which to be fair, when you're young, it often is. He presented this plan as if it were a revelation, and presented it with some urgency, and emotion, before turning back to tales of sixteenth-century Cossack assassination campaigns. I tried to contextualize this within the framework of romance even as there was something slightly clinical in his approach. That night he started to ask how I was feeling, and I noticed he'd stopped drinking and was applying new restraint to his diet. When we docked in Hvar, he insisted we visit the iconic monastery. It was dark, and I could barely see him standing a few feet away, his hand pressed against a fresco on the wall, muttering under his breath. Was he praying?

I had walked to the altar, passing pews filled with nuns, and when I turned around Marcus was gone. I called his name, and one of the nuns held her hand out, offering a small paper prayer. I accepted it, thanked her, then walked outside to find my new husband sitting on the stone steps, staring at the sun.

"Look what the nuns gave me." I thought it would amuse him.

It was The Lord's Prayer, printed on light green paper barely thicker than an onion skin, English on one side and French on the other. Marcus held it in his hand for a long time, then passed it back to me, as if I might need it more than he did.

"It's the key to the garden," he said, finally, and I knew him well enough by that time to track how his mind moved like that, always expecting you to keep up.

"I know," I said.

"Maybe you will bring back those roses. I wouldn't mind."

He took my hand and wiggled the platinum band.

"I love you," he said. And then, "I'm dying."

And then slowly, so slowly, as if pulled by an invisible thread, he stood. He looked across the square. I didn't know what to say or think when he broke the silence with the one line I thought couldn't possibly come next.

"And that's not all."

III

LOBSTERS

The thing is, my parents *liked* chaos. They invited it. In the presence of chaos, they felt important, engaged, I think. It was only much later that I learned, as all children learn new things about their parents once they've grown up, that there were other elements underfoot in my childhood home, aside from the money running out, as it always was, aside from my father's serial history of career failures—as my mother put it—his "Olympic lack of ambition." There were secrets. When you grow up in a house of secrets you get very good at keeping them. Without understanding what it meant, somewhere along the line I had developed what Marcus might have called a "casual relationship" with the truth.

You might think, given this, that what I loved about Marcus was what seemed to be an openness, a what-you-see-is-what-you-get transparency. Marcus never snuck around a corner to make a phone call. Marcus left his bank statements out on the kitchen counter. Marcus, at least the Marcus I knew in those early weeks and months, seemed to live with a kind of radical openness, at least on the surface. That surface was an act and a defense, though I didn't think much about it all until later, chalking it up—if I even thought about it—to his capacity for distraction, his need to be busy. Marcus always had so much "going on," as he put it, a fact that felt exhilarating to me. You can easily conflate business with success if you've grown up with a father who spent most nights staring at the wall. Having watched a father with nothing to do, it felt safe to be with a man who never stopped to stare at anything.

On our first date Marcus had asked about the white streak in my hair, a birthmark I had tried to hide as a child but that had become so much a part of me I had sort of forgotten about it.

"I can color it over," I had said, "if you don't like it."

"Oh, but I love it," he said. "I think you should make it brighter."

"They used to call me 'skunk' at school."

"I like it. And I love you."

He had also asked about my childhood, my family, if I had ever traveled in France or spoke any languages. I hadn't and didn't. He asked if I liked art, and what kind of art, and showed me some images of paintings on his phone. They looked like enormous exploding flowers.

"What do you think of these," he had asked.

"They're very violent."

"Yes, they are."

Marcus loved art, and he loved history even more. Marcus claimed he liked old things, but his hunger for the new belied that. He claimed to know very little about contemporary painting, though later I would learn that he had lived with a famous painter for years. People defined by their contradictions take time to know. Some are liars, others simply lack self-knowledge. And a third category, the rarest, are the people who cultivate contradiction as a way to deflect intimacy. I remember thinking that everything Marcus told me in those early days was a way of bringing me closer. That it was love, seduction. That, finally, he did want to be known. It never occurred to me that those early days were in fact a kind of test. A school with one teacher and one student. The one being known, then, wasn't Marcus at all. It was me. "How did I find you," he said, many times. "Thank God for you." As if he'd finally found the solution to a problem he had spent years trying to crack.

*

"You can see the Louvre in six minutes," Marcus said. We were in Paris only days after leaving Dubrovnik. We weren't in Paris for the Louvre, though, we were there for a meeting, which Marcus had explained in the car on the way to the hotel, related to "a new project."

I had never been to Paris.

Marcus spoke flawless French.

"Six minutes sounds fast," was all I said, as the car passed the Louvre's glass pyramid. "Do you even get to go inside?"

I wasn't thinking about art at that moment, though. I was thinking about the last forty-eight hours and everything he'd told me that day at the monastery. I was thinking about *The Year of Magical Thinking,* the book that Marcus had left on the bed for me, and how Didion put it, that when life changes, it changes in an instant. And how important it is to stay calm, to show less emotion, because life is just catching up, in the end, isn't it. Life is *hurry up please, it's time.* I felt showing less was what Marcus wanted. I could be the brave wife. I could be, one day, the brave widow. These are the things you tell yourself at the entrance to the slaughterhouse. You can't know, yet, what the threshold is.

You can't know at which moment it will be too much and you'll cry out for help. And so there I was, feeling courageous, as we sped through the streets of a city I had only read about in history books, a city my mother claimed to have loved. A city in which it was almost impossible not to engage in magical thinking.

"Paris is for lovers," was written on a coffee mug she used for her afternoon tea.

We had not come to Paris for love, though, had we.

We had come to Paris for work, for the "new project."

"You will be great," Marcus said, squeezing my hand.

Outside, the Tuileries.

And as I closed my eyes and tried to remember everything that he had told me on the plane, what I was meant to say at the meeting, how I was meant to respond when asked certain questions, how he would be leaving at a certain point and I would be left alone with the others; Marcus was talking about Napoleon and Petain, about the "unbroken" history of narcissism evident in former French leaders. How "Narcissism is almost essential for a Frenchman" and how "Even in the retreat from Moscow they all *dressed* so well." Marcus behaving adamantly as if everything were normal.

"Yes of course you go inside," he said, now holding both of my hands. "You see the *Mona Lisa,* for five minutes, then move on to the *Winged Victory,* for one."

"What about everything else," I said.

"There is never enough time for everything else."

The Louvre in Six Minutes, I would understand, was the description of a mission for Marcus.

Precise, controlled, always oriented toward the goal.

That day, in that car, I had accepted a few things. That the man I loved was dying. And that he was not the man he had pretended to be when we met. This was all weirdly all right because, in disclosing the truth to me that day outside the monastery, in inviting me into his trust, Marcus had offered me the real thing I had fallen in love with him for: a new life. A life of color, risk, of *doing things,* things that matter.

"How do you know I can do this," I had asked.

"How does a brain surgeon identify the origin of a tumor," was his response. "You were born for this," was how he put it.

As our car slid around the perimeter of a vast stone courtyard leading to the hotel, Marcus took his hand away from mine and my cheek. I was wearing a simple dress he had given me that last night on the boat, sunglasses that had mysteriously appeared in a small silk pouch on my night table, and my wedding band. It was perhaps, looking back on it now, my own armor for whatever battle I was about to encounter. Marcus told me many times not to be afraid and that all I had to do at the lunch was listen. Then he wanted to know if I had eaten enough, and what had I had for breakfast. The night before he had brought a steak tartare to me around eleven, "a midnight snack." I told him I couldn't possibly eat it, so he sat on the edge of the bed and ate it himself. He had given up smoking after we had talked about a baby, and in place of nicotine had taken up caffeine, which he ingested in the form of Red Bulls and chocolates and which I didn't mind as it took his edge off. This new habit made rest scarce, though, which seemed by design. He did not want to lose a moment to sleep. He did not want to close his eyes. With the empty plate between us on the bed that night, he had lain down next to me and told me he loved me and that he knew "I was the one," and that he was proud of me. The last thing I remember before falling asleep was that his eyes were open.

At the entrance to the hotel he said, simply, "Thank you."

"For what?"

"For trusting me. Nothing matters more than trust."

Inside the hotel Marcus led me to a large dining room, which was entirely empty except for one man seated alone at a corner table. Waiters closed the restaurant's wide double glass doors behind us as we entered and, as we got closer, I noticed two, then three, four, finally five men in dark suits standing against the far walls.

Yes, this is my dress, I told myself. Yes, these glasses guard eyes sensitive to light following a childhood accident. That's why I wear them inside, please don't interpret it as rude. Yes, this diamond bracelet was given to me the night I met my husband. We met at an art opening at the Tate Modern in London, and I am an aspiring art dealer. And no, I do not have a gallery yet, but that is my dream. I have plans to work with a small set of exclusive clients, and will start with a few friends of Marcus's, he's been so generous in making introductions. I will work through word of mouth, no social media, no "brand," I am a club without a number on its door.

This was the story I was instructed to tell: I was an artist. I loved watercolors as a child. I loved Monet. I worked at Giverny summers during boarding school, then later studied at the Uffizi in Florence during my first year at university, where I learned old master techniques, "and the difference between a liability and an asset." From the time I was nine I knew that I would one day have a life in art, only I couldn't afford at first to be on the creative side of things. I was born poor. School on scholarships, benefits (this all came easily as it was close to true). And then by the time I was eighteen I realized what I actually loved was business, *markets,* the complications and emotions attending transactions, deals, competition. The *game* of art as much, in certain ways, as the artists.

What I want is to help artists as well as clients, which I believe is possible. My clients will be the people who understand that the essential value in a work of art is how it makes you *feel*.

"And tell him about last week," Marcus had said, the night before, previewing how things would go.

Yes, right, *just last week* we were at the Portrait Gallery and Marcus was so bored because "royals bore him," but I didn't want to leave the room with Ditchley's Elizabeth.

"And when he asks what you admire about the painting, remember to talk about her power."

What I *admire* about Ditchley's Elizabeth is how Gheeraerts depicted her as she was in all her power. How the absence of a child, or a husband, was less a flaw than a choice. How, in his mind, which happened to be the truth of the matter, Elizabeth held all the cards. In never letting anyone truly know her and, in refusing to commit to one match, that was the essence of control. And power. Power can come from holding back. Elizabeth understood the value of risk, I would say.

"Risk is highly underrated," Marcus said. He had taken his shoes off and was staring at the ceiling. It was nearing midnight and I was tired, but we were not quite finished. "Say something like that, that risk is underrated."

"I would never say something like 'Risk is underrated,'" I protested, but Marcus maintained that he knew "our audience," and that this was a very good line.

And so, by the time I entered that dining room that day in Paris in the small hotel in the sixteenth arrondissement I could speak as eloquently about old masters as I could about contemporary art, for example Jeff Koons, whose factory I had visited just the other day to bring flowers to his assistant on the occasion of her birthday. She likes peonies, real ones. She wants to be a painter herself one day, too, but what better way than to "learn from the master."

You see, there was a script.

And if you had studied it closely you would see Marcus all over it.

His voice, his wit, his bent for irony.

He would teach me all of these things and they would become mine, for a time.

Annabel assisted. Annabel, who had appeared on the boat the night after our day in Dubrovnik, and who told me more about what she'd meant by the use of "sphinx." Annabel, and the file Marcus handed me after dinner that night. The file had nothing written on the outside but on the inside was everything I needed to become the person I was about to be, the person he needed me to be, as he put it, "briefly, unless you like being her, in which case you can keep putting her on." *Keep putting her on*, as if he were talking about a glass slipper. Glass slippers are very pretty, but glass breaks.

"What is this," I had asked, opening the file.

"*This* is how you're going to save my life," he had said.

Marcus, that night in Dubrovnik, had explained exactly what was going to happen over the coming days and weeks and months. He had it all planned out almost to the hour, and my role and choices within the timeline were already decided. My role was explained as "a favor," and as "simply doing the right thing," as if that were obvious. As Annabel put it, "Wouldn't anyone do the same?" In fact, by the time he'd explained what was about to happen, about to change, I was so completely in Marcus's thrall I never thought to question what "right" meant. What was laid out before me, then, felt less like a risk than like a promotion. I was being invited into something very special, *important*. He was handing me an identity I had been looking for without even knowing it.

Most people take a lifetime to find themselves.

If someone offers you the answers—*who you are, where you come from, what you want*—you might simply say thank you. Especially if those answers exceed anything you could have dreamed up on your own.

As we approached the table, the man stood.

"Raja," he said, extending his hand, which I took. "I am so happy to meet you," he added, with a level of intimacy that didn't bother anyone. Raja nodded approvingly to Marcus as if I were the student who'd just aced the exam. Marcus leaned over me, dipped a piece of bread in olive oil, and said, to Raja, "Knock my socks off." Though at the time I thought he was talking to me.

Raja was Lebanese. Marcus had told me Raja was the son of a celebrated scholar whose books preached reconciliation in the Middle East, and whose life had been threatened on multiple occasions in the wake of "terror coming on the scene," in the seventies. Though terror had always been on the scene, hadn't it. Marcus and Annabel had explained to me that Raja's only flaw was his belief, like his father's before him, that he was always the smartest man in the room and, as Marcus put it, "The smartest man in the room is not always right." Annabel added that Raja's charisma was something to mind closely, as it tended to catch people—women and men—off guard.

When I asked what Raja did "for a living" the phrase seemed to amuse Marcus. Raja was, Marcus told me, a liaison between the Lebanese government and foreign "investors," which in retrospect was true. Marcus told me that he was looking to expand his investments in Lebanon and so now needed Raja as an ally and guide. Marcus said he and Raja had met in London, as "youngish" men, not long after Raja had finished university, and that Raja had been planning a life between Paris and Byblos, "because he loves beautiful things." When I asked why I needed to pretend to be someone I was not to meet him, Marcus said he would explain later. And when I pressed, he simply kept coming back to trust. If I *trusted* him, it would all be fine. If I *trusted* him, one day I would understand. If I trusted him, I would see he wasn't asking me to do anything unethical.

And then he would take me to bed, and everything was complete and right and clear. I was still a kid in so many ways. I was up for games. I had no idea that a world existed in which people played the kinds of games that were dangerous. I had no idea that there was a difference between a fairy tale and a lie. A fairy tale might break your heart, but it can't kill you.

"I don't feel like myself," I had said, looking at my image in the mirror in our hotel room.

"You look perfect," Marcus had said. He ran his fingers through my hair.

"Are we playing a joke on him?" I had asked.

"No, we are doing him a favor."

At the lunch, wine we hadn't ordered arrived, poured silently by a waiter Raja clearly knew well. No one touched it, though, as the men talked of things entirely foreign to me like the price of oil and arbitrageurs, about friends of theirs who had "retired" recently and about a trip planned, but never taken, to Saint Petersburg last year. The waiter delivered a first course no one had ordered either, asparagus with diced egg on top. I had never seen anything like that, nor would it have occurred to me to pair something as horrible as asparagus with something as sublime as an egg.

"Nothing is new," Marcus had said. "There is nothing you haven't seen before."

And so I looked at the dish as if I had eaten it a hundred times.

"What's essential is to appear natural," Annabel said, as she showed me how to knot my hair into a chignon.

"Confidence," she said, "is a weapon."

Confidence, confidence, confidence.

The word became my *there's no place like home.*

Like Dorothy, I was headed toward Oz.

Marcus's phone rang just as I had devoured the last bit of egg. He excused himself, and the real meeting began. Raja started by asking simple questions, how Marcus and I had met, where I grew up and had been at school, had I had time to see the new show at the Musée d'Orsay. Eventually, as I had been told that it would, the interrogation's scope crept to the personal. Was I close to my father? I told him, as instructed, that both of my parents were dead.

"You're an orphan," he said, leaning in, "like me."

The game was intimacy. The game was the cultivation of trust.

He told me he had long ago stopped believing in family and, as he said it, I could feel his eyes lock onto mine like precision guided missiles. Their absolute bright blue. Raja was, I thought then, one of the best-looking men I had ever met, and perhaps this was what Annabel had meant by charisma. I wanted not to be off guard, but being confronted by someone with that kind of beauty makes it hard to breathe, you can't help but feel awkward, like they know you're admiring them, like they are used to it and bored by it and live for it, all in equal measure. Was I really about to tell this man a series of lies I had been trained to deliver with poise, design, and assurance.

Confidence, confidence, confidence.

Pretending is not a crime, it's an escape.

He told me how he'd been a boy playing football near the U.S. Marine barracks on the day of a bombing in Beirut, "before you were born," and how that day crystallized a desire to "do something meaningful" in the world, which he said he was sure I could understand. He told me about the British soldiers who had driven him home that day, how his mother had prayed for "the dead Americans and their families," how his mother had loved America, perhaps why both of Raja's wives had been Americans, too.

"Do you have children," I asked, as two enormous boiled lobsters were laid in the center of the table between us.

Two tiny silver dishes of butter were placed by our forks, and Raja watched like a hawk as I broke off one lobster's tail, sliced a line carefully down its center with a knife, then skillfully pulled the meat out in one piece. I dipped it generously in the butter and ate it with my hands, like an animal, just as Annabel had showed me. Where was Marcus. It felt like hours since he had left. I continued to eat, as Raja watched, in silence. The waiter replaced the used lemon slices. I noticed Raja nod to the men standing by the wall and watched them file slowly out of the room.

And just like that, we were alone.

"What did Marcus tell you about me."

"He said you are an old friend."

Which made him laugh.

"What else."

"He said you like beautiful things."

"True. What else."

"Nothing else," I said.

I was getting good at the lies.

Raja explained that Marcus had told him a little bit about me, and about the business I was hoping to build, "So impressive, at such a young age, to be clear about who you are and what you want." Raja told me that one of his "very dear" friends was living outside Paris and was a very "important" collector with a very special collection. He told me this friend was giving a lunch there in two days and that he, Raja, was unable to attend as he and Marcus would be tied up with other business, but that he hoped he might send me in his place. That I would love these people and, even more, appreciate the chance to see a collection that had "largely been hidden from the world, a private commission" of unusual scale and scope.

"I assume you can swim," he said, and I nodded, and he told me, "Don't worry, there are no sharks there, at least not in the ocean."

I asked if his friends were French, and he explained that the husband was "a mutt," and that the wife was "a white Russian," though I had no idea what that meant. And the wife had a daughter from a prior marriage—"The girl would be around your age now"—who was called Nikki, and that Nikki would be at the lunch. "And there is a young boy, whom they homeschool at the moment." Raja explained that the boy was the father's son from another marriage, and as he went into some detail about the nature of the "compound" I started to think that maybe the way I was raised, while brutal in aspects, had a level of simplicity. I was on another level now.

"It would be a personal favor to me if you could meet my friends, this family, get to know them. And then we will have lunch again and you can tell me about your time there. How does that sound."

Everything that day might have fallen into the category of "ordinary things," and yet I would soon understand that nothing about this was normal at all.

He placed his hand on my wrist and said, "I will not forget your kindness."

And then Marcus was suddenly at my side, apologizing for being tied up and distracted, telling me all the ways in which he would make it up to me. He waved to the waiter for the bill, which made Raja laugh. I would learn that no one picked up the bill when Raja was around. As Raja stood to go, he looked right at me but spoke to Marcus.

"You're a lucky man, Marc."

I watched him exit through the glass doors.

Did he look back at me, almost imperceptibly?

The shift of his head an inch to the left.

In that split second and with that shift, I recalled tracing the outline of a heart on a London bus window when I saw another man. It was before Marcus and Paris and lobsters. It was a different me.

Marcus leaned in to kiss my neck.

I didn't think about what I had seen or remembered if I had in fact seen anything at all.

I rarely looked closely at things then. I rarely connected dots.

Someone looking closely and connecting dots would have noticed Marcus had returned from the gym that morning having not even broken a sweat. And so might have asked where he had been. Someone less trusting than I was might even have followed Marcus that morning to discover that he had gone not to the gym, but to meet Raja. The two men had talked about their lives, Marcus with the knowledge his was coming to an end. And it was a very different Marcus that morning, a Marcus without pressure to perform, relaxed in the presence of someone who knew him so well. A Marcus stripped of the armor, and the story, he had needed to be with me. Alone with Raja, walking Paris streets, Marcus was simpler, gentler, far less brash. He was at peace with the choices he had made and where they had led him. At peace in the knowledge that something was coming to a close, not just his life but his life's great work. If I had been able to listen to their conversation that morning, I would have fallen even deeper in love with him. It was ironic that he did not need to be who he thought he needed to be for me to love him. That irony cut both ways.

That night after a long walk we returned to our hotel. Marcus was weaker. He had lost weight in the last days but refused to talk about what was going on with his health, and I didn't pry. We lay in bed, and he placed his head on my chest.

"You know I need you, don't you," he said, and I did.

Do we know when we make the choice that changes everything?

I would learn, eventually, that nothing about Raja was ever casual, nothing in his life ever went off script, unless by design. I would learn he was less a fixer or liaison than a soldier, that in fact he had been one of the most highly decorated military officers of his generation, and that his expertise was not arms, though he could handle himself on a range. His expertise was espionage, a field that required a fine mind, a tolerance for risk, and, above all, emotional intelligence. Espionage is seduction. Your first experience of espionage can feel a lot like falling in love.

By the time we reached Paris, a stripping away had begun. Marcus had started paring down his life, preparing to let go. The vicar came off the payroll. The finca went on the market. "Let it all go," he said on the phone within earshot, he wanted me to hear it. "Give it all away." There would be only one thing he would hold on to. And with that choice he was not only laying a clean path for his exit but also preparing me for what was to come. And for what would come after.

*

Cap Ferret is a slim peninsula off of the Atlantic coast of France, bordering Arcachon Bay, which, until around that day when I first visited, had been primarily known to and inhabited by fishermen, surfers, and a few special Parisians whose friends in Bordeaux let them in on the secret. It was not a place for tourists, or celebrities. It was, and is, a place for family, for summers of long naps and walks to the Dune, for handpicked oysters with *vin blanc*. Cap Ferret was the perfect place for hiding in plain sight.

You can take the train from Paris, or drive, either of which seemed perfectly acceptable options, but two days after the lobster lunch Marcus drove me to a nondescript office tower in La Défense, the business district of Paris, where we rode a glass elevator to the roof. From there, you could see the entire city. The Eiffel Tower looked weirdly small. I had never been at that altitude.

Marcus held my face in his hands, and I was sure he was going to say again that he loved me but instead he said, "All you have to do is listen." He walked me under the whirring blades, opened the door, and even placed the headset on my ears, then kissed me on each cheek and said, "See you for dinner." As he jogged away across the landing zone, he didn't look back.

I had never been in a helicopter. The experience of moving up, fast and vertically, was new to me. As my ears popped the pilots offered champagne, but all I wanted was to take in the view. Flying over Paris, I thought about my mother, who would have loved being surrounded by so much beauty. And about my father, who claimed to have climbed mountains in his youth but who I knew was in fact afraid of heights. I thought about their lives and the life I was living now and wasn't sure whether I felt pride or shame.

Soon we were moving fast and low over the Paris suburbs and across the countryside until I could see, in the distance, the sea. The pilots pointed things out along the way, but in my head all I could hear was Raja talking about "my dear friends." About how I had, after lunch, gone with Marcus to a salon that looked more like a small museum, where a man who spoke no English didn't mind that I spoke no French as he explained to Marcus what he planned to do to me, gesturing to my face like I was a doll. Marcus knew what he wanted. He even showed the hairdresser a photograph that I didn't see. And then he watched, amused, as the man removed enormous gleaming scissors from a red leather case, washed my long hair twice, combed it, then brought me to the chair by the mirror, where he proceeded to take off six inches. Looking in the mirror I thought about the Ditchley Elizabeth, and about control.

The helicopter paused, hovering over what appeared to be an enormous log cabin the size of a small hotel. We were only meters from a bluff overlooking a private beach, which stretched for about a mile and seemed, perhaps as it was overcast, empty. Or maybe it was the hour, not quite noon. "There," said one of the pilots, and I followed his gaze to the left out the window and could see, hidden among a kind of small wood, a landing pad discreetly painted the color of its surroundings. As we moved closer, I could see a woman walking along an allée of linden trees leading from the house to the helicopter pad. She wore a white swimsuit. She was barefoot. Though I could not see her face, if I had been forced to guess I would have said she was forty, and I wondered if this was the woman Raja had spoken of, "the white Russian." As we came closer, as the helicopter touched gently on the ground, and as the woman removed her sunglasses, I could see she was young. She was maybe a few years older than I was. She opened the door and held out a hand to help.

"Welcome," she said. "I'm Nikki." And I suddenly felt awkwardly formal in my suit, with my new hair, a fraud encountering the epitome of authenticity. It would never have occurred to me that she, too, might be putting on an act, an identity for my benefit. That she, too, might have been told what to wear when she met me, as to the significance of a white swimsuit; instructed as to the quality of confidence communicated by bare feet or impeccably messy hair. The meaning of casual warmth. She had what I assumed at the time was a cool acquired from being born into something special. Into a line. Into access. For the first time in a long time, I wished I could blink myself back to my flat in London, to being alone and on the outside, to no risk. Only there is no such thing as no risk.

Only we can never blink ourselves back.

Nikki thanked the pilots and asked them in for iced tea, but they declined. As she led me along the path through the allée of linden trees toward a lawn, on the other side of which was a set of stairs leading to an enormous stone door, two dogs fell in alongside her.

"Hansel and Gretel, meet my new friend," she said, in subtly Russian-accented English. And to me, "These babes are the true owners of this place. Belgian Malinois, trained killers, don't piss them off."

As she walked ahead, I could see the helicopter move up and out over the beach. And as my eyes dropped to the water, I saw three men driving jet skis in a slow line along the coast, perhaps a silent patrol. I remember glancing at my phone. And, as a feeling somewhere past fear and before panic started to rise in my chest, Nikki turned around and looked at me.

"Very hard to catch a signal here. You're welcome to use the house phone."

I said nothing, which is to say I answered according to Raja's Second Rule: *less is more than more. Less is an invitation.* Raja had said this in the hotel, while we rehearsed, just before Marcus and I left for La Défense. I would run through my cover story and then he would give me hints or lessons. Rules, gentle guidance, theories of the case. Like a tailor with a suit, Raja had made sure the fit of the story was impeccable.

"An invitation to what?" I had said.

"To fill the silence."

And then, looking especially approvingly at my hair, he took a slow, deep breath. As if I was a relief. A solution to a long-standing problem.

A key, a path, a resolution.

I was none of those things, though, was I.

I was a Hail Mary, an Ave Maria, a last chance.

IV

ARCACHON

At the base of the stairs leading to the entrance of the house, three men in black T-shirts held silver trays with lemonades, and champagne. Nikki, who had just explained—"it's short for Nikita, which means 'winner,' and my mother likes winning"— took one of each then walked up the stairs, the dogs at her side, and onto an enormous porch lined with antique rattan chairs and wooden chinoiserie drop-leaf tables. She drank the champagne in one sip then set the glass on a table and told me she thought we could start with a tour, then meet "the family," and then eat. She was mindful of the fact that I would have to leave in a few hours. As I followed her, a football team's worth of children appeared seemingly from nowhere, raced past me, and started to play tag on the lawn. As we moved through an enormous hallway anchored by palm trees (a tree indoors!), I saw, among other things, a woman nursing a newborn, teenage boys playing chess, three older women in swimsuits reading on chaises longues, and a few other, much older men I assumed, by their uniforms, to be staff. They carried platters of food through a door at the far end of the room, which led to another outside space. Through the door I could glimpse a pergola.

Pergola. Chinoiserie. Chaises longues. These were not words I was familiar with then, but looking back now I can see the house so clearly. And now I have the language to describe it, not only the furniture and the people but the emotions. Looking back, I see it clearly. The house to me at the time seemed filled with family and love and excess. The children at play.

We entered a wide white kitchen where Nikki picked a deviled egg from a tray and popped it into her mouth. She kissed the cook, who wore matching white terry wristbands and a U.S. Open hoodie with the sleeves cut off. It was freezing. I noticed enormous brass buckets filled with wine bottles, which, it occurred to me, could bring the whole house down if they were to ice over and explode.

After the kitchen came a library, then another parlor, and finally a back porch off of which I could see another, separate structure, one I hadn't noticed from the air. It appeared to be an architectural folly, circular and made entirely of white stone. It felt completely out of place next to the house, which, while large, had a casual, almost Caribbean feel.

"This is my stepfather's museum," she told me. "A museum of one. One artwork, one visitor, one patron." As we approached, I noticed a small electronic keypad by the door.

Barely caring that I was watching, Nikki entered the code and the door, like an elevator, slid soundlessly open. "I know," she said, "it's silly, but my mother is obsessed with security, it comes from having been kidnapped as a child." I let that land without pressing; Raja had told me that part of my role was not to be curious. Inside, eleven enormous canvases hung from ceiling wires, each placed inches from the round walls, giving the impression of a kind of three-dimensional experience. You could walk behind the canvases, or in front of them, between them. I had never seen art displayed that way, and as I got closer, I noticed wires running from the base of each canvas down to the floor, too, preventing the paintings from moving. The wires were so thin you could only see them if you stood inches away. Otherwise they were invisible, and the canvases seemed to float in thin air, each at the exact same height, spaced precisely apart from the walls and from one another. The structure, then, had been designed and built specifically for them. Stepping into the center of the space you were completely surrounded by the art and, as I started to look more carefully, I understood that this was a kind of series, all done by the same artist, and that the series told a story.

A story of slaughter.

Nikki explained that her stepfather was contemplating selling the paintings because he had, in recent years, gone partially blind and the idea of this art he so loved but could no longer see clearly had started to depress him. She told me the paintings had been commissioned, that her stepfather had asked the artist, "Tell me the story of the *Iliad* and the *Odyssey* in emotions," that what I was looking at was the first half of the project. That the artist had died before he could complete it, "which is a pity, as what you see here is so much about death. You get the war, but not the peace, which might be a perfect metaphor, if you know Edouard," she said.

Nikki walked to the far side of the space, which, if I had to guess, was around two thousand square feet. As she moved, tiny floor lights linked to noise, or perhaps to heat levels, illuminated to further focus the eye on each canvas.

"Helen, Paris, Menelaus, Hector, Patroclus, Priam," she said, like a child counting dimes for a candy purchase. "At first Edouard thought of commissioning a series of artists and asking each one to consider a different chapter in the story, which is of course very episodic, but then we worried that everyone would compete for the bloodiest bits. Every artist loves a battle. So I convinced him to let one artist do the whole thing. Edouard flew to Rome and took his favorite painter to dinner and, well, Edouard is very good at persuading people to do things for him. It took him six months to say yes, and then we all went to see them in his studio before commissioning an architect to dream up the perfect space to hold them all. During that time, we moved here, and my stepfather decided this would be the place to house the paintings. It was his idea to have them live in the round, he felt it was . . . democratic. And that it would make you feel immersed in the experience of the story. Come, look."

The floor was one large slab of limestone. Nikki moved to a small wooden chair—the single piece of furniture in the space—to wait while I looked carefully at each canvas. I asked if I could take notes and she said no but that if, after my time today, I decided to work with the family, to help with the sale, I could come back and take as many notes as I liked. And then it was clear that I was not there to see if I wanted the job. I was there for the family to decide if they wanted to hire me. Even though Raja had assured me, "There is only one candidate for the position," I suddenly felt like I was the art under inspection. That the table had turned.

"I know why he wanted *you*," she said. "Do you?"

"I am good at my job," I said, and she laughed out loud.

That was Nikki's curse and her blessing, a confidence that slipped easily into condescension.

"I am sure you're *very* good. You're very pretty, too."

And just like that, something shifted. Was Nikki reminding me I wasn't there for deviled eggs, I was there to provide a service, to play my part. What did Nikki know? She walked closer to me. She was so close I could smell the champagne on her breath.

"I don't bite," she said, baring her teeth.

She urged me to take all the time I needed—"We'll eat in an hour"—and as she closed the door behind her I wondered if there was any way she could lock me inside.

My phone had come back to life. A single text popped up, from Marcus: *I love you.* And I wrote back, *I love you, too.* I closed the phone and spent a few more minutes admiring the paintings. What I loved was the use of color and white space. How could anyone put a price on something like this? The images were abstract, and not necessarily identifiable. Some looked like enormous flowers mid-bloom and others almost like grids of reds and purples and golds. Only one painting had a clearly identifiable human figure in it, a woman. She wore a crown of brightly colored jewels, which, on closer inspection, might have been a crown of thorns. Each canvas contained letters or phrases around the edges, but they were too abstract to read. They were written in many languages.

"Everyone will welcome you," Raja had promised, when he came by the hotel before we left. Marcus was calm, tired, and hadn't touched his French toast. He lay on the bed in his slippers while Raja paced the Persian carpet and ran through the questions one last time with me, actors running lines.

Where did you study?
Florence.
Be specific.
The international school.
And your focus was. . . .
Use of color in the Renaissance.
Like what colors.
Azurite. Ultramarine. Indigo.
What else.

Verdigris. Malachite.
What was the role of color.
To create the illusion of dimension.
To fool the eye.
No, not exactly.
What then.
To enhance the experience.
Of the viewer.
Yes.
Do you have a favorite artist?
So many. Too many.
Oh, but if you have to choose.
Titian. Twombly.
And where were you born?
England.
Be specific.
Outside Oxford.
Be specific.
Burford.
Where are your parents?
Dead.
How did they die?
A car crash.
Was it an accident?
I don't know. I think so.
Do you miss them.
Yes, of course.
Did you love them.
Yes.
What did they teach you.
Manners.

What else.
To keep an open heart.
Try again.
To learn more about the world.
Good, yes. And how did you meet Marcus?
At the V&A, an opening.
Which opening.
Decorative Arts of the Napoleonic Era.
How old are you?
Twenty-five.
Twenty-five but an old soul, right?
Yes.
You've been told you're an old soul many times.
Yes.
Are you on social media?
No.
Why not?
I'm an old soul.
Why else.
I like privacy.
Who are your clients.
I don't think I can tell you that.
Will you sign an NDA?
Of course.
And how did you meet Raja?

How did you meet Raja?

How did you meet Raja?

I was told that if this last question came up, not to answer, that the absence of an answer *was* the right answer, that discussing Raja was the one thing that would always be off limits wherever I went. It was that morning in the hotel in Paris that I finally woke up and understood that Raja was exactly what you, by this point, have likely deduced. Yes, Raja may have been a skilled diplomat, and decorated soldier, he may also have been the son of a great man. He may have possessed an ability to love, and he may truly have loved Marcus, at least. But Raja was also a ghost, a cipher, the lie you need to save yourself. A designated traitor in certain markets and a calculated killer in others, the human analogue to another missile strike. Raja would claim, if pressed, to be allied to no one, only ever to "the mission." This wasn't true, though. In the end everyone is allied. As you cook supper or walk your children to school, as you navigate the ordinary emotional rules of life, Raja knew ordinary life was as much a fiction as any "cover" story. Ordinary life for Raja was a set of chess pieces without names, of longitudes and latitudes, of "enemies" whose histories of poor choices Raja was committed to setting right. Buddhists live in the moment. Raja lived in game theory.

Raja was a spy.

A spy in full, entirely incapable by the time he met me of ever looking back at the boy he once was. Raja, like Marcus, like all the ones who last in his line of work, had fully inhabited his cover, and it suited him. The line between who he pretended to be and who he really was had, by the time I met him, almost entirely evaporated. Once, Raja had been a dreamer, a romantic, a boy looking for an exit from his life, for meaning. Raja had been a good son and an observant child, well-mannered to a fault thanks to a mother he was deeply keen to please. The son of an arrogant father, prone to casual abuse as a result of his own shame, Raja longed for a way out, longed to be the operational shot caller in an important game. Raja, once, had been a lot like me.

"We want one thing above all," he said, repeating himself, as if talking to a child, which in a way I still was. "We want to know if the father, Edouard, is in the house, where exactly he stays in the house, and where he goes if he ever leaves, who he sees, who he does not see. We want to know everything you can learn about him." And there it was, the end of the story that started with "And that's not all" that day at the monastery near Dubrovnik. The end of the story was not an epiphany or a glass slipper that fit. It was a two-letter word—"we"—indicating Marcus was involved in all of this, too. "We" was more than Raja, though, far more than Marcus. "We" was weapons grade, nation state, fully funded. "We" was a network operating at a level I didn't even know existed, nor could have imagined it. "We" was the small set of people who ran the secret world from their glass-walled conference rooms in Arlington, Tel Aviv, and Vauxhall. "We" was in the very serious business of doing the jobs no one else wanted to do, and of finding the right assets on the ground to assist in any mission, Berlin to Bangkok to Bagram to Beirut and in between. And while most new intelligence recruits never sign a formal contract, I had. And while most new recruits don't recite a vow, I had. My vow was simple, a rite of passage in any ordinary life: *in sickness and in health, till death do us part.* Any asset can leave her handler, but I wasn't any asset. I wasn't recruited by a case officer. I was recruited by my husband.

"All she has to do is enjoy herself, listen, have a nice lunch," Marcus said, his eyes closed, as if in penitence. As if that were the whole truth.

And that was when they started to argue. Marcus was worried about me and worried about Raja forcing me too far, but looking at them, it was clear who was running things. At one point, Marcus looked at me and said, "You don't *have* to do anything at all," which, if I had been older, if I had seen more—if I had *read* more, maybe—if I wasn't as naïve and inexperienced I would have understood the classic line that always comes from the good cop in the good cop-bad cop scenes. The good cop is there as a foil, and to make the mark feel safe. The mark, me. What the good cop-bad cop scene does is give the mark confidence that she will be cared for, that at least someone is on her side. The good cop-bad cop scene is designed to elicit confession, or inspire choice. In my case, the latter was the goal. They needed to know I would do what they wanted. They needed to know I would be good at it. And they needed to trust me. By the time I had boarded the helicopter, I was completely clear on what I was doing, and why, and for whom. I felt a level of pride, even of cool, as if I had been given the lead in the school play. Farce, romance, comedy, tragedy, problem play. I didn't know the genre yet. Intelligence assets, like actors, are often shown only those scenes in which they will appear. What I told myself was that I was doing this for my husband. What I told myself, and believed, was that no one would get hurt.

*

Lunch was a long table set for forty, give or take a few, under the pergola. I was seated next to Nikki's mother, Dasha, with a boy of about ten on my other side who told me his name was Aleksandr—"with a *k*," but that he went by his middle name, Felix—"with an *x*." He barely stopped talking as plates were laid down the line of the table, meats and cheeses and small pots of butter and jam, freshly sliced mango and melon and multicolored carrots "from the little garden." Felix said that he liked English football and did I know any footballers? I broke the news that, sadly, no, I did not, but that my husband might know a few, and should I ask him? The boy wanted to know which teams I liked so I lied and guessed, saying Arsenal was "all right," which resulted in him giving me a brief history of the various clubs and their rivalries, like a historian expounding effortlessly on War of the Roses arcana. Down the table I could hear French, English, Spanish, and what sounded vaguely like Arabic, all being spoken interchangeably, a Tower of Babel on the beach.

Dasha said nothing and ate in silence. Children eat quickly so, as the younger ones finished, they left to return to their lawn games, at which point Dasha turned to me. She looked very young, but I would guess, given Nikki, that she was in her late forties. Dasha led with "elegance, and cultivated curiosity," in Raja's words. He warned me that Dasha was suspicious of everyone, having lived a life in the "shadows," but said that my age would defuse the bomb of her concern. "In her eyes," he had said, "you're like a child, and as she was a child bride herself, she might even feel empathy, or whatever she can access closest to that." She wore the simplest white shirt over a swimsuit, no jewelry, no makeup. This family, on this day, appeared happy and engaged, immaculately inclined away from perfection even though everything they did was, in my view, perfect. Millions of dollars of art housed less than a quarter of a mile away, attack dogs asleep lazily on the lawn. I worked hard not to acknowledge any exoticism in it all, pretending as if this was how I spent every day, pretending I was one of them, or might have been. As if perhaps I still could be.

"Where are you from," Dasha asked, pulling grapes casually from the enormous purple bunches that lay in a line down the center of the table. Two garden roses in tiny glass vases set by each place reminded me of my garden, our garden, of Marcus and the prayer bench. That garden felt very far away now. When would I be back? And would we even return to London? That day on the boat the one thing Marcus had been clear on was, "We are going to spend some time around Paris," and I didn't question him. He'd told me he wanted to see some doctors working on an experimental treatment for his illness which he described as "neuromuscular, degenerative," and not treatable, and when he didn't say more than that I didn't press. He told me that he also had a "bad heart," with an irregular beat, that he might have a stroke any day if he forgot to take his medicine. "I'm an old man," he'd said, as if it were his fault.

"I'm from England," I told Dasha. "Near Oxford."

"Where near Oxford, I know it well."

"Burford."

"Ah, lovely, near the water."

"Yes."

"And were your parents professors?"

"No, they were"—at which point Nikki sat down on my other side, taking Felix's seat. She had brought her plate of meats and cheese with her, intent on joining the conversation.

"How do you know *Raja*," Nikki said, it was less a question than an indictment. "A far more interesting question than if your parents taught university."

My parents hadn't gone to university.

"I met him through my husband," I said.

"He's a recent acquisition of Nikki's," Dasha said.

"It's true."

"Raja is no one's acquisition, I can assure you."

"That's not fair," said Nikki.

"My grandfather was blind at the end of his life, too," I said, trying to pivot. "A silver lining was he learned to love music. By the time he died he knew as much about Tchaikovsky as your son was just telling me about Turkish football."

I nodded to the boy on the lawn, who I knew was not her son but her stepson.

"My husband loves Tchaikovsky," Dasha said, which I also already knew.

"I like *Swan Lake,*" I said.

"Edouard loves *Swan Lake.*"

And then she said, "My husband will never sell those paintings, even if he goes completely blind, but my husband loves meeting young, beautiful women, so we have welcomed the distraction of your visit today, a distraction I believe was"—and she glanced at Nikki—"your friend Raja's true intent."

And then one of the staff was by her side, explaining with some urgency that she was needed. I asked Nikki if everything was all right, she assured me it was, and asked if I had time for a swim before I left. As we walked away from the table, I could hear someone say, "If America dies, she will die by suicide," and then, "You know who said that? Lincoln. Abraham Lincoln."

Nikki led me to a guest bedroom, where a blue swimsuit, in my size, lay on the bed, the price tag still attached, alongside a towel, swim cap, and goggles. On the floor was a new pair of sandals, also my size. I changed and looked at myself in the mirror and remembered Marcus as he licked the icing from my finger, the Komodo dragon robe, and "Happily ever after." I felt, in that moment, complete confidence that this was all completely normal, meant to be, by design. Life leads, you follow, is what I told myself. On a desk, I noticed a lacquered box of light blue stationery. Rather than a name or address, a quote was printed in tiny, elegant block letters across each sheet:

IN THE HOTEL OF DECISIONS, THE GUESTS SLEEP WELL

Turning it over I could see the same phrase was written, in French, on the other side:

DANS L'HÔTEL DES DÉCISIONS, LES CLIENTS DORMENT BIEN

As I walked into the hall, I noticed Dasha emerge from a few doors down then close the door carefully behind her. She walked away from me toward the stairs, never looking back, but I could feel she'd noticed me, and I wondered if I had already overstayed my welcome.

"All we need to know is if he is there," Raja had said.

"And if he plans to stay," added Marcus.

I walked to that door. As I came close, I could hear music inside. As I leaned in, I recognized it. *Swan Lake*. Marcus had taken me to see it in London, on one of our first dates.

Carefully, I turned the doorknob, which clicked, and the door opened. And, making up what might pass for an excuse in the event I was caught, I walked into the room and almost into yet one more Belgian Malinois. He looked up at me and gave a low growl. I stood completely still while the music played. That night after the ballet, when Marcus and I made love, he had taken his time, more than before. I remember it feeling like he was trying to make up with me, even though we hadn't argued.

The bed was unmade. Books were piled on the coverlet, as

well as a laptop, four mobile phones, and a breakfast tray with the remains of lunch. The little garden roses in their vase, the grapes, a small dish with chocolates. I could see a door on the far side of the room and walked toward it. The dog didn't move, as if he trusted me, as if maybe he was there to protect me. There was a sofa piled with papers at the other end of the room, and as I walked past, I could see documents in many languages. Glancing into the bathroom, I noticed the sink was dripping, as if someone had only minutes before finished washing their hands, or shaving. Men's cotton pajamas lay in a heap on the floor. As I turned to go I saw an enormous map hung on the far wall, framed in Lucite. As I got closer, I could see the map was printed on silk, that it was what I would later learn is called an "escape and evasion" map, used to plot routes into, or out of, hostile territory in wartime.

The map showed the far eastern border of Turkey, into Western Iran, and was dotted with tiny red lines and markings in what looked like Morse code, dots and dashes. The map appeared to have been torn, and so only this part of it remained recognizable, though the paint was bright, as if it had been recently restored. It was its own work of art. Was this Edouard's room, Edouard the blind man? Edouard, the ghost. Edouard, the husband and father, *step*father; Edouard, allegedly the architect of crimes, the center of a horror story no one had told me yet. Edouard, the one to watch. Edouard, the man I was sent here today to find.

When I had asked Marcus who Edouard was and why Raja was interested in him, Marcus said, "He's the king of kings," then said not to ask more, not yet. He did add, "If he *is* there, which I very much doubt, and if you do meet him, he may want to spend time alone with you. And if that happens, don't be afraid."

I remembered Nikki's comment about the paintings, about having the war but not the peace. I took a step closer to the bed.

I wanted to see what the books were, and just as it struck me as odd that a blind man would cover his bed in books, I heard a noise from downstairs, the dog barked, and I rushed into the hall, closing the door behind me quickly. I thought I had heard something, or someone, inside the room, but I was at risk of being late. Even then I could safely conclude that Nikki wasn't one to abide lateness.

She was waiting on the beach, which was half sand and half rock, and as soon as she saw me, she ran into the ocean and dove under the first large wave. I joined her and we swam silently out for what felt like a long time. The water was warmer than I had expected.

"I like you very much," she said. "You must come again."

We treaded water and looked at the shore for a minute. And then she dove back down, and I could see her swimming fast back to the beach, as if she were racing. A small cabana had been set up, inside of which, on a chair, were my clothes and my bag. "The helicopter is here," Nikki said as I emerged from the ocean. Of course it was. The entire day, including my exit, had been choreographed far in advance of my arrival.

And as we approached the landing pad, Nikki kissed me three times, left cheek then right then left again. My hair was still wet as we lifted into the sky, which was the clearest blue. I looked back over my shoulder, away from the house and even farther from the small round museum. I could see a clearing in the trees and, inside the clearing, I could barely make out a lap pool, its dark water well camouflaged by black walls. I could see someone was swimming laps, naked, wearing only swim goggles. It was a man. At the edge of the pool, another man sat silently smoking, dressed in a suit, as if keeping watch. The swimmer reached the edge of pool, the end of his lap, and, just as we were rising up away and out of view, I thought I could see him raise his head and follow the line of our flight.

"On y va?" said the pilot. "Home?"

"Yes, please," I said. "Take me home."

V

KING OF KINGS

As a helicopter lands, you feel like you're floating. And, briefly, suspended. Looking down out the window, I could see the rooftops of La Défense, and thought about the thousands of people working in those buildings, engaged in transactions that gave their lives meaning, transactions that placed food on their family tables, work they might hide from their wives occasionally in the event that this or that deal required privacy or discretion. Required "confidentiality," a word that could as easily mean the stakes were high as it might mean that the partner on the other end of your husband's mobile phone was a woman, and an attractive one, and you might not want to bring that fact home and into your bedroom.

There is always the risk of accidental insinuation, in certain lines of work. Certain lines of work require different rules. I remember thinking, as the helicopter touched down as gently as a butterfly, that it would not have awakened a sleeping baby. I remember thinking about the levels of secrecy most people are willing to endure, if they are honest people, and how for most it isn't much. Not because we are saints but because secrecy is something that takes strength. If you had asked me when I was younger, I might have said that a temperament inclined toward secrecy was probably a temperament inclined toward anomie, atheism, even a belief in an imminent apocalypse. An inclination toward secrecy implied amorality. I really had not thought about all that before, until the Cap and those canvases exploding with color, their elegant abstractions. I had not thought about what secrets I might be capable of holding until I admired those grapes laid out along the table, Dasha's perfect, simple shirt. Perhaps as I had not thought before about who I could be, and be happy as, about the kind of woman I could inhabit who was and was not me. In that quiet moment, looking over the endless rows of windows not yet dark for the night, that was my view.

Raja, not Marcus, was waiting on the roof. He wore jeans and a navy cotton sweater, which made him seem casual and made him look young, a foreign exchange student out for an afternoon stroll across the rooftops of Paris, no big deal. As I bent to run under the blades and toward him, he lowered his sunglasses with a forward tilt of his head, and I could see those blue eyes, and he smiled, as if he already knew what had happened in the last hours and was pleased about it all. Or, perhaps, as if it didn't matter anymore, maybe he was simply happy to see me, maybe I hadn't failed. I pulled back my still-wet hair into a knot and stood there awkwardly, the girl at the dance waiting to be asked for the first foxtrot. If there was shame in that moment there was excitement, too. What was next.

"Hey," he said simply, and then put his arms around me. "You all right?"

"I'm fine, absolutely fine."

It was a gesture entirely out of keeping with the man Raja had been that morning, not twelve hours earlier, his performance of borderline brutal interrogator, demanding professor, rageful boss. Now Raja had transformed into something else. This new man led with warmth. "Just think of him like a slightly mercurial older brother," Marcus had advised about Raja. "His moods will shift, but his loyalty holds."

Raja said Marcus wasn't feeling well. He said Marcus had asked him to come and collect me and take me for dinner—"And please make her eat," is what Raja said Marcus had said, which sounded like him. We rode the elevator down in awkward silence, and he walked me to a waiting car. I thought I felt his hand touch the small of my back, but when I glanced down his hands were firmly in his pockets, another very Raja pose that made him read younger than his years. He was forty-five, then. Forty-five, though when he was twenty-five he was equally capable of very serious things. When he was my age.

"How was it," he said, again with a kind of preternatural gentleness, absent any of the earlier stress.

"Fine," I said. "I think."

"How was the ocean," he said, as if he hadn't heard my joke, or as if it wasn't very funny.

"Warm."

"The coast is beautiful, isn't it."

"Yes." And there it was, those opening lines, how Marcus set the table, laid his cards. How he opened every conversation to establish the mood of the scene. The rough stuff would be out tonight. Simplicity would be in. Kindness.

We drove to the Musée Rodin, Hôtel Biron, in the seventh arrondissement, a place I knew about as Marcus had told me he'd like to get married there but then, as he was prone to do, he bought the place in Mallorca and changed his mind. Marcus had scrolled through images of the Hôtel Biron on my Instagram account, as of course he didn't have one. Was it odd Raja was taking me to a place I had not only been shown images of by my husband, but which had been the planned location of our wedding? In fact, if Marcus and Raja were so close, why wasn't Raja there that day in Mallorca? The thing is, when you open a new door in your mind everything can seem unclear, up for new interpretation. I had, without even knowing it, been conditioned to keep my doors not only closed but carefully locked.

"I've booked the little café," Raja said, and we walked around to the back garden where the small outdoor space was empty except for one or two couples having a late cup of tea; it was still way too early for anyone in Paris to think about dinner. As we entered the room I noticed one of the women looking at me, and I felt ashamed of my messy hair, which moved along easily into shame about a host of other things, like my general ignorance, like why hadn't I been taught about things like Rodin, like did I even learn anything at all in school. I knew nothing about Auguste Rodin, only that a poster of the sculptor's iconic work *The Kiss* had hung in the room that had once been my mother's bedroom. It was the only piece of art in the house where I grew up, the romance of it in contrast to the entirely unromantic atmosphere of my childhood. My mother loved it, though, a fact that—those doors in my mind opened —struck me as a coincidence.

Raja looked at me.

"Tell me. Tell me about it."

He reached a hand across the table and placed two fingers around my wrist. This gesture was a reminder: *I set the stakes.* Or was it a dare. Was it saying *go ahead, pull away, see what happens.*

I didn't move.

He passed his thumb across my wrist, back and forth like a windshield wiper, then pulled away and sat back. A waitress brought two plastic glasses of champagne. Raja said he wasn't hungry yet and asked me to walk in the garden.

He said nothing for a long time. And then, once we were away from the café and he had finished his champagne, he—finally—said quite a lot. He had assessed it was time. That assessment is something you're trained very carefully for. Asking someone to commit espionage is like asking someone to marry you. You only ask once, and you only ask when you're certain of the answer. The ask is an expression of power, which is why with marriage it's traditionally been the man who asks, on the presumption that the man has the power. The power, the confidence, whoever has that is the one who sets the rules.

"What do you want to do with your life," Raja asked. "Have you thought about it at all."

"I don't know," I lied, because if pressed I might have said that what I wanted was to have a child, be a mother, that I had not thought too far past those things.

"I would like very much if you would consider working for me."

"Working for you doing what?"

"Exactly what you did today."

"And what exactly did I do today?"

"You listened, observed, remembered."

"And lied."

"Yes, that's also true. You're good at it, though. How did it feel?"

A young couple walked along the path toward us.

They laughed and admired the view.

The woman put her head on the man's shoulder.

The man put his arm around her waist.

Raja let them pass.

"There goes ordinary life," he said. "Is that what you want?"

"I think so."

"I don't. I don't think ordinary life is your style, my friend. An ordinary girl wouldn't go for someone like Marcus. Ordinary girls don't accept offers to spend their days pretending to be someone they are not."

"I did that for Marcus," I said, which felt like a plausible stance.

He moved closer.

"You are the perfect person for a complex job we have been working on."

"Who is 'we'?"

Raja looked up, as if God would take it from there, as if God even knew what he was thinking.

"Well," he said, " 'we' is the United States government. The Central Intelligence Agency. CIA. And 'we' have been looking for Edouard for a very long time."

"Why?"

"I can't tell you that, yet." And then he said, "You remind me of me, at your age."

"You and I have nothing in common."

"We're both optimists. We're both orphans. Espionage loves an orphan."

And we walked on, and Raja told me more of his story. What he said was that he had been recruited to work for the British intelligence service, MI6, while studying languages at the American University of Beirut. What he said was that he had spent his entire adult life in "the secret world," enjoying the sense of mission it provided, "Having grown up mission-less, if that makes sense, it's always ones like us who end up drawn to the mythology of it all, our one shot at adventure." He told me how his English professor recruited him when he was seventeen, and how the professor later handed him over to another, more senior member of the service, a successful businessman operating under what Raja explained was called "nonofficial cover." That business-man became Raja's handler, his runner, his case officer. His men-tor. That businessman invited Raja into the closest thing he had ever had to a family.

"He was, then, younger than I am now," Raja said. "He seemed so old to me, he seemed to know everything."

The businessman, Raja went on, had work that required fre-quent travel into "all sorts of very complex places, which made him the perfect spy. He could go anywhere without being noticed, without coming under suspicion. Like you did today." Raja told me that he entered "service" when everyone truly believed the Cold War was over. And how the "new wars," then, had begun. How it was once rare, before the century turned, for a banker to go to places like Baku. "Most bankers like linen napkins," he explained.

"What was the banker's business," I said.

"The kind that makes you a bloody fortune."

It turned out that despite all his talk of myth and romance, Raja was ruthlessly practical. Raja was happiest in rough towns and dark corners, but matter-of-fact when it came to the elements of craft. Elements like violence. Raja was anesthetized to violence. Raja didn't care for linen napkins. As "places like Baku" became new centers of capital, as the definition of "exotic" changed and when what was once "the third world" became simply "emerging markets," which is to say, opportunities, the secret world evolved, too. In an era of radical transparency it became harder to slip under the radar. The radar was everywhere. You had to acquire new skills in the new era, one of which was to be as comfortable in five-star restaurants as in war zones. That was Raja. Raja, who would claim to hate the theater like an Olympic athlete complaining about exercise. Theater is essential to the secret world.

Everything I had assumed about Raja before that night was wrong. What I had seen in the large dining room on the day we first met was an assay, a come-on, an introduction. Now we were down to the business of the thing. Like he said, you only ask once. You only ask when you know the answer. At the time I knew as much about espionage as I knew about Chinese foreign policy. I had an idea that it was complex. I didn't know, then, that espionage is simply human interaction performed under exceptional circumstances. The game of espionage, at its essence, is observation, seduction, patience. And a fluid relationship with your sense of self. To commit espionage at the highest levels you have to be willing to forget who you are in order to inhabit someone else. To perfectly mimic the emotions of a recovering addict, for example, or a grieving widow. Queen Elizabeth, Joan of Arc, an Olympic archer. It can be learned, like any other skill.

Raja talked about his childhood in Lebanon. He asked if I had ever been there (even though he knew I had not). He wanted to know if I had any sense of Beirut and whether it was a "good or bad" place, if I had ever read any books about or ever studied the Middle East in school. And what about Russia, and the Soviet Union. What about the Cold War. Did I know the relationship of Russia, for example, to the Middle East, and did I know anything about the history of my own country in the region. I said I had known Lebanese twins growing up, in London, how I had visited their house down the block where their mother cooked classic Middle Eastern meals, lamb stew with raisins, chicken laced with pomegranates. In other words, I knew very little. He told me that the Cold War had never ended. He told me Edouard was once a general in the Russian army, and that he and Edouard had met when they were stationed in the same place, when Raja was a young man. Edouard, Raja said, was rumored to be descended from the Romanovs.

Russia, to me, meant the Russian nesting dolls my mother kept on her dresser.

She kept her engagement ring inside the smallest one.

"Russia," my mother once told me, "is romantic."

Russia, to Raja, meant corruption, deceit, slaughter, betrayal.

Raja had never shown me any identification to prove that what he had told me was true. Nothing to prove that he had been working as part of a "special mission unit." He told me he had done one thing, and only one thing, for the last nine years.

"Which is what," I asked.

"This," was his answer.

He said the operation was nearing conclusion and that I had arrived "for the last act."

"The last act is the most important," he said. "It's the one people remember."

He told me he had spent a decade in Lebanon before, unexpectedly, being transferred to Tehran. He told me he grew to love Iran, the people, the landscape, the language. And that, just as he was beginning to map the rest of his life there, only weeks after he'd fallen in love with a professor of Iranian literature, that businessman had shown up at his flat and said, "There's been a change." The businessman told Raja that Iran had just been training for a larger job. By that time fluent in Farsi, Raja would return to Beirut, where his new cover would be as an Iranian agent recruiting assets on behalf of Iran. Raja would join an elite joint CIA-MI6 operation. The operational goal was to develop a new network of assets in Beirut.

"What about the professor," I asked.

"It was a promotion," Raja said. "I really couldn't say no."

"Lebanese, pretending to be Iranian, working for America."

"*And* the British."

"And the British."

"Correct."

"Did you ever wonder who you were, under all of that?"

"No."

"And the lying."

"It's the job."

The sun had set.

Raja never asked the central question again, he didn't have to, I had already provided my answer.

I was in.

He put his hands on my shoulders.

"This is a calling," he said, "like the priesthood. It's a question of faith."

He dropped me at my hotel and, as the doorman opened the door on my side, looked straight ahead and said, calmly, "It's a good thing, to save lives. It is a good way to spend a life."

*

Marcus was not in our room. The bed was made. A small silver tray lay on top of the sheets holding a supper that had not been touched, a bottle of water, a bottle of wine. I could feel my heart start to beat faster. I called out for Marcus but before I had said his name twice, I was already in the bathroom, and he was there on the floor, and he was no longer breathing. In his hand, a piece of yellow legal paper, the kind my mother used for lists and goals, was folded perfectly in half. I opened it:

RAJA WILL TAKE CARE OF YOU.

And my phone rang, but I didn't answer as I went to call the hotel operator and ask for an ambulance, please, and then within what felt like minutes that ambulance arrived with a raft of men who took Marcus away, and I was asked to sign papers, and give a statement. I was asked if I wanted to come to the morgue, or if I wanted "assistance," a euphemism for pills. A woman appeared, claiming she worked "with the hotel," and offered to place phone calls, were there not family members I needed to call, or perhaps people who could come and comfort me, help me, death is a complex business. There was only one person to call now, and he wasn't there. There was only Raja, the one person on whom I had, in an instant, become entirely dependent. Raja, whom I had elected to trust as well. Raja who arrived within an hour and patiently waited while I wept, slept, raged. Raja, who wore his sunglasses inside, like a movie star, until I realized he was wearing them to conceal his own emotions. Raja, with his hands deep in his denim pockets and his long game, who looked at me that night with what certainly felt like deep care. Raja, who was in mourning not for a husband but for the man who, as he had done for me, had changed Raja's life, been his mentor, his friend, the closest thing Raja had ever had to a father, a brother, a family.

In the morning, I woke up in my clothes to the smell of coffee and eggs and bacon, Greek yogurts and melon and berries, nine kinds of tea from which to choose. Raja sat at the little desk doing something on his phone. I looked at him for a while until he turned around, smiled, and said, simply, "Hey." I wanted to ask him never to leave, and yet, without saying anything, what emerged in that moment was not a question but an answer. By the time Raja moved to sit next to me on the bed, by the time I

had placed my head on his shoulder as if he could fill the emptiness that had defined me for so long, as if he alone could make
the sadness go away, by that time I had said yes loudly and clearly
without saying anything at all. Yes, to the proposal made in the
Rodin garden. Yes, to mission and lies and risk, games and meaning. Yes, to *the priesthood*. Yes, above all, to not looking back.

VI

JACK AND JILL

When I woke up, it was evening. Someone was knocking on my door. I opened it to find Annabel, who embraced me warmly, and said she had come as soon as she heard the news. She noticed me looking around and she told me Raja had gone to work, that he would check in later. She said some "other friends" were coming by, and it was then that I realized maybe also Annabel was not the person I had believed her to be. Annabel was a sphinx, too. Annabel, if not a part of the secret world, was adjacent to it. Annabel, also, would be part of the third act.

Annabel went to the phone and ordered room service, steak frites for four.

"You have to eat," she said. "You need your strength to play the young grieving widow."

"I am a young grieving widow," I said.

"And that will make it much, much easier."

Another knock at the door. Annabel answered and a man and woman entered. They looked vaguely familiar. Had I known them growing up, or met them before with Marcus? The man put his hand out; he had the longest fingers I had ever seen, and wore rings on four of them. He also wore the kind of cashmere tracksuit CEOs at that time found cool, but he didn't look like a CEO. He didn't look older than thirty. His hair was cut militaristically short. He had an earring, a tiny cross.

"Bubble, bubble, toil and trouble," the man said, kissing Annabel on both cheeks. He looked at me and said, "I'm Jack. What's your name, new girl?"

Jack went to the minibar and removed three Cokes. He handed one to Annabel, one to the other woman at his side, who drank it ravenously, then offered the last to me. The woman looked even younger than he did, maybe twenty-five, though it is always hard to tell. She wore a very short skirt and had insanely long legs that dropped, miles from her hips, into worn Tretorns. She was eerily, impossibly tall. As Jack sat on the bed as if he owned the room, she folded herself into one of the tiny French chairs by the window, chairs Marcus had looked at and wondered if they'd been "built for dolls." Her hair was platinum, reinforcing the feeling that she was the kind of girl I had known, but never been. The kind of girl who stands out, an exotic beast, an alien. She leaned casually back and, barely moving, slid the blinds closed with one arm. She was strong.

"And this is Jill," Jack said, gesturing at the alien. Jack's accent sounded Irish, but an Irish tamped down by years spent in cities far away from Dublin, or Belfast. It was an accent I associated with movies my father loved, stories of immigrants, gangsters, people proudly on the outside. Jill, when she finally said something much later, sounded Slavic, though I had never heard of a Russian called Jill. She was from Ukraine, raised in Odessa, on the Black Sea. She had been a soldier in the Ukrainian special forces. Jill and Jack had had many incarnations in their time as "partners." Jack had been her brother once and could speak flawless Russian. He had been her husband at least twice, and the kiss always looked real. Jack and Jill liked operations with no drama, but if a distraction was required, they could fight like tigers in the middle of Paddington Station, Charles de Gaulle airport, the Tiergarten. Jack and Jill were not their real names.

"You were a *pretty* bride," Jack said, and then I remembered. Jack was "David, from the office," in Mallorca, the man who'd said the thing about Marcus not making everyone sit through *Macbeth*. "Is it true you ate the cake before the wedding and that was why we had to fly, like, two hundred crème brûlées in from Madrid?" He looked at Jill and winked. "Crème brûlée only flies first class, baby."

"It was an accident," I said. "The cake."

"I don't believe in accidents," said Jill.

The only thing Jill believed in was cash.

Annabel removed a silk scarf from her bag and spread it out on the bed. Painted on it was an elaborate map which, after a moment, I could see clearly was the compound at Cap Ferret. I could see the house, the beach. I could see the pergola and the landing pad. The pool.

"What is *this*," I said, admiring the map's beauty.

"Escape and evasion map," Jack explained, then pointed to a small dotted red line that ran from the main house across the sand over to a rocky bluff. "This will be easy, this is not Sanaa. In and out, streamlined, low cost. Just the way the Mothership likes it."

"The Mothership likes success," said Annabel. And to me she added, "The Mothership, Uncle Sam, the Americans."

The Americans. And yet there we were, a Brit, a Ukrainian, an Irishman, and, as far as I could tell concerning Annabel, a Swiss or possibly a Dane, though it would turn out she had gone to Yale, which was where she was recruited. Espionage, at its essence, is borderless. In the days leading up to Arcachon, two decades

into the twenty-first century, the old rules and systems of intelligence had broken. A level of order had evaporated, the old orga-
nizing principles of the business obliterated by technology, cyber,
the death of cash. A new style was forming to take its place. And
yet the new style was, in some ways, the oldest style of all. It was
analogue. It was silk maps and handshakes. It was no phones, no
dead drops, never write a memo. In the new order, the availabil-
ity of information was the degradation of information. And yet
while operations like Arcachon appeared streamlined, they still
required what Raja called "state-sponsored insurance," a fancy
way of saying planning, and cash. Every lie I would tell in those
days was subsidized and green-lit by someone I would never meet
whose security clearances were known to only a handful of senior
government officials, speaking of Russian nesting dolls. In the
new style, it was precision and deniability *über alles*.

*

That evening in the hotel there was very little keeping me in
place except trust. The role Marcus had played in my life and the
need, then acute, of holding on to that. I had never dealt well
with death, and Raja had assured me what Marcus wanted was
"nothing, no memorial, no fuss," that he wanted to be cremated.
Maybe he simply wanted to disappear. Marcus always knew what
he wanted. The absolute absence of doubt in his life was inversely
proportional to its constant presence in mine.

I told myself the choices I was making were simply a matter
of survival.

I would follow these people not in the service of a government, but in the service of myself.

Jack smoothed the lines of the silk over the bed and pro-

ceeded carefully to walk me through what "we" knew so far. The
level of detail he had about the house was impressive. About the
house as well as about all of its inhabitants. I was only beginning
to have the sense that outside the world in which I had lived, the
civilian world of bricks and mortar and social roles and certainty,
there existed another, parallel world defined by its architecture
of surveillance, deception, and lies. Defined by "covers" and evasion plans outlined over room service in three-star hotels. A world
of coded language foreign to most civilians. And yet the entire
system of smoke and mirrors did have a goal. And that, to me,
at that time in my life, was enough. How each choice had to be
precise. How every decision had to move the ball forward.

Jack laid a small square piece of butcher paper next to the
silk onto which he had crudely outlined a floor plan for the compound's main house. Next to that he placed a series of grainy
black-and-white surveillance photographs taken from the air.
Each image had two tiny letters stamped at the bottom, next to
the date and time. "EO," which I would learn means "eyes only,"
a funny phrase indicating that what you are looking at will not be
seen by anyone else. Or at least, that's the goal.

"The house," Jack said, pointing to the butcher paper, "sleeps
eighteen, if you include the children's rooms. It was designed to
maximize discreet exits and minimize entrances. We believe he
stays upstairs most of the time, probably *here* is my best guess,"
he went on, and pointed to a square marked "MBR1." Master
Bedroom One. It was the room along the left side of the second
floor, the largest such space in a line of perfectly square spaces. I
had experienced it all as so casual when I was there but looking at
it more closely, I could see clearly the care taken with the design.
The way the pergola served less as a design element than as protection from, for example, attempts to surveil meals from the air.

"Who is 'he,'" I said.

"Edouard," said Jill.

"Then that's not right," I said.

"What's not right," Annabel said.

I pointed to the room I had walked into, where I had heard the music.

"I think he sleeps *here*," I said.

"How do you know that," said Jill.

"I saw Dasha leaving *this* room so—"

"Dasha's movements indicate nothing," Jill said.

"It doesn't matter," Jack said. "*A*, if they're smart, and they are, he moves around and doesn't sleep in one place for more than a night, that's the shell game with the rooms, otherwise what are all the rooms for, it doesn't make sense. And *b*, ideally, we won't be entering the house. I don't like simple homes, and this one's a maze. Look at this." He pointed out a hidden elevator.

"The children are a problem," said Annabel.

"Yes, way too many children," Jack said.

Which, it turns out, was also by design.

The children were the real security system at the Cap.

Jack looked at me. "Knowing more about the children will be helpful."

I thought about the boy who loved football.

If he knew any of this.

If his bedroom had a back balcony with, as Jack put it, "excess egress."

Jill pointed to a circle on the map.

"Chapel," Jill said. "They're Russian Orthodox, right?"

"It's not a *chapel*," Jack said. "It's a safe house."

"No, it's for his paintings," I said.

"Well, it's built like Fort Knox," said Jack. "The shape, the absence of windows. And the fact that it appears to have a base-ment, which could easily include a tunnel. So, we *do not* want to end up there."

Annabel lit a cigarette.

"This whole thing needs to be outdoors."

"Correct," said Jack.

After that night, I would never have a meeting with Jack that lasted more than ten minutes. After that night, I would never see Jack perform any typical human task. I would never see him write anything down. And I would never learn his name, if he was mar-ried or single, rich or poor, if he liked men or women, if he had anything at all in his life outside of this. And I would see that that level of obsessive devotion to work was one that I not only recog-nized but one that I envied. In that way, it was a question of faith.

"We know the family eats lunch together every day, usually outside, usually *here*." He pointed to the pergola. "They can actu-ally enclose it with temporary walls." He laid a black-and-white photograph on the bed, and there it was, the pergola. Seen from above it looked more like a bomb shelter.

"This is what your life looks like on paranoia," Jack said, and laughed. "Only Russians would do this. Israelis? They just keep their guns on the table."

"Who cooks," said Annabel.

"They have a cook," I said. "A man."

"Any man there is probably part of the detail," said Jill.

"Everyone is part of the team," said Jack. "Everyone except the children."

Jack explained how a single, mile-long road led in and out of the compound. He explained how they had purchased the prop-erty from local farmers who had held it for generations. And how Dasha and Edouard's names were not linked to the property, nor was any Russian corporation, nonprofit, government office, or intelligence service. "But," he said, "our formerly Soviet friends always, always, *always* leave a little Easter egg in the trail so that, if the right person is looking, you will always be able to confirm it was them."

"They can't help themselves," said Jill. "They have to remind you how smart they are."

"The LLC they set up in the stepdaughter's name links to a mobile phone guess where."

"Probably not Dublin," said Annabel.

"*Beirut,*" Jack said, smiling. "Game, set, match."

And he tore up the photograph, and the butcher paper, and folded the map neatly into his pocket.

Annabel turned to me. If it wasn't clear before, I suddenly understood that she was the one in charge. A kind of hierarchy was taking shape. Raja was leading and, under Raja, Annabel gave orders to Jack. And, if you wanted Jack, Jill would be part of the package.

"You need to try to talk with as many people as possible," she said. "Staff. Guests. Anyone you casually run into on the beach. We need a clearer sense of who is there full time, who comes in and out regularly and why. We need to know if they have a plan to relocate and, if they do, to where, and when, and how."

"They have a French-speaking detail. That way they can speak in other languages and no one can track what they're saying," Jack added.

"What other languages," I said.

"Algerian, Chinese. Farsi," said Annabel. "Russian, of course." Jack's phone buzzed. He looked at it.

"We're late," he said to Jill, and they were gone.

There was no handshake, no kiss on my cheek.

There would be no more pretensions of friendship.

Annabel sat on the bed and motioned for me to sit next to her.

"It's a lot," she said.

I wasn't sure if she was referring to the meeting we'd had just had or to Marcus's death, probably both.

"All we are asking you to do is listen. Marcus knew you would be perfect at it."

"What is the goal of all this," I said.

"We don't really talk about goals. We talk about process. We talk about tactics. Goals are above my pay grade, and yours."

"Why was I sent to talk about the art."

"We needed someone to get inside that structure, see what it was, if it really held paintings."

"Or what."

"Or other things."

"Well, it was," I said. "For paintings."

"Every killer was once someone's baby boy, or girl."

She stood to go, then turned at the last minute, her hand on the doorknob.

"Dasha and Edouard are married, but they were never in love. Nikki is Dasha's daughter from another marriage. And Felix is Edouard's son from another woman."

"Is there anything else," was all I said.

"Get some rest."

I fell asleep in my clothes and immediately launched into dreams. In the only one I remember, I was me, only taller, as tall as Jill, and growing taller as the dream evolved, with these endlessly long legs and increasingly freakish height that let me see over the tops of everyone's heads. A truly new perspective on the world. I was a mountain.

And I was walking in what felt, at first, like a kind of rain forest but then I realized I was back in Marcus's garden, my garden, my garden, our garden, and I could see the meditation bench up ahead, and the low, long pond. I could hear Marcus, somewhere just out of sight, clearly singing lines from a song he, ironically, loved even as it described something that he was entirely incapable of— "Slow down, you move too fast, you got to make the morning last." And I could hear him, and I kept moving closer to the voice, but I could not see him. I thought the voice was just behind me. I could almost feel his hip grazing mine, the way he would pull me into him.

And yet when I turned around it was not Marcus. It was the little girl I had seen all those years ago, in the garden. She was all grown up and yet wearing a white dress like the one she had worn that day, her hair pulled tightly back into a braid, her shiny shoes. She was singing, but with Marcus's voice. And as I looked at her, she suddenly was not the little girl from my past, she was me. I was looking at myself having become this other thing. And inside my tall, tall body, inside the alien that was the other me, I tried to bend down and touch the girl, prove she was real. I took a step in her direction. And then what sounded like a gunshot broke the dream open and I was alone in the hotel, the white ceramic ceiling fan slowly spinning above me. The shot wasn't a gun, it was the latch in the door. I sat up and there he was, Raja. He must have had a key. Of course he did.

Without turning on a light, he sat on the edge of the bed, facing away from me.

I waited for him to say something until, after a few minutes, I realized he was crying.

"I loved him, too," he said, not looking at me.

"I know."

He turned and looked at me.

"Dasha was once a young widow, just like you. She was married to a celebrated Russian military general. She likes men who make her feel safe."

"Most people like to feel safe," I said.

He started to pace the room, like a lion, as if it were perfectly normal to have a meeting, or whatever this was, in the middle of the night.

Nothing was normal anymore. Nothing would ever be normal.

"And yet, what matters even more than safety?"

I said nothing.

"Dasha knows loss and that's why she will understand, or think she can understand, what you're going through. Do you remember everything you learned today."

"Yes."

"Your story is that you asked me to find a private place, for a week or so, for you to gather the pieces."

"Pieces of what."

"Pieces of you."

He looked out the window.

"Dasha owes me a favor, and I'm collecting."

"Why do I want to be surrounded by strangers."

"Because you have no one else."

And then he said, "And Dasha knows what that feels like, too."

The clock on the bedside table said 2:00. The time. Time was real, an unalterable fact. What else was, until now, real and not real. Had Raja chosen me for this at the wedding. Or was the choice made earlier, and was it Marcus who chose, at that party in London. Or was there someone watching me even earlier, maybe on the day my parents died and left me an orphan, the perfect prey. The orphan who likes the garden. And then she happens to meet the man who bought it. If accidents don't exist, what do you call that?

Fact patterns, as lawyers like to call them, are only linear in retrospect.

You can organize a fact pattern to ally with any version of the story.

You can organize a fact pattern to condemn a man to die.

"We will pay you," he said.

"I don't want anything."

And he laughed.

He said he was having some things delivered for the trip.

"Clothes, gifts for Dasha and the children."

The helicopter would leave from the same place, La Défense, at ten. He removed a tiny, simple phone from his pocket, the kind of phone I associated with children or with drug dealers, a phone meant only for texts.

"This is *only* for me. Call on this phone and I will always answer."

And then he was gone.

I tried and failed to get back to sleep and into that dream, back to Marcus. Was I simply moving through someone else's paces now, making choices I would have never made if Marcus were alive. Was I myself, or was I still in shock, and was that all part of some larger design. I closed my eyes and remembered "sleep is the only thing that won't go to bed with me" and how Marcus would assure me that "if you lie quietly and close your eyes, you will get ninety percent of the rest you would get with deep sleep." I did not understand that Marcus must have had many nights like the one I was having then. Lying awake, thinking through choices. I closed my eyes, and I could see the man swimming laps in the

Cap pool, looking up at me. Was that Edouard. Who is Edouard. And what had he done.

*

The luggage consisted of two enormous dark green leather cases with my initials embossed in tiny gold letters. I opened one to find, on top of a few perfectly pressed linen dresses and several silk nightgowns, an envelope with my name. Inside was a card on which someone had scrawled, in ink, "Bon voyage" next to an image of a multicolored hot air balloon. There was a small terry cloth makeup case with my name on it. A hairbrush and comb, two toothbrushes and toothpaste, floss, various face creams and blush, deodorant, ibuprofin. A simple leather wallet contained three credit cards and five hundred euros, a new passport. And also, something I had never seen before: a marriage license. My marriage license.

I could see my name, and a signature that looked like my signature, though I had never seen or signed this document, though no one had ever said anything about a license. The vicar and the Shakespeare, the cake and the dress and the vows, that was what the marriage had been. When I had asked about a license Marcus had assured me "the Spanish are so laid-back," and that "the vows make it legal here." He said we could find a British clerk, later, to finalize the details.

Under my name there was a name I didn't recognize, on the line for "husband:" TARAN DAVIES. Attached to the back of the certificate was a small envelope inside of which was a series of photographs: a smiling Marcus, smoking a cigar, on a sailboat. Marcus and me at the entrance to the monastery in Hvar, holding hands. Wedding guests on the lawn in Mallorca. And me, in my white dress. Someone had written in bright blue marker with Marcus's inimitable scrawl, "I love you forever, T."

My phone blinked.

It was Raja.

"Listen carefully," he said, as if he knew what was going through my mind in that moment, which was, how far away, and how fast, can I get on five hundred euros?

Raja told me one of the children from the Cap compound had been sick the night before, and that it was serious enough for the child to be flown to the Hôpital Saint-Louis, in Paris. He said the car would collect me at the hotel and drive directly to the hospital, where I would sign in to visit the child "as his godmother" and then escort the child in another car. He said I should plan to spend twenty minutes, no more, at the hospital. And then he hung up.

I opened the car door to find an enormous stuffed teddy bear upright in the backseat, a blue satin ribbon tied around its neck with a small white card that read "Pour Felix."

Felix, who liked football.

Felix, who played with his friends on the lawn.

Felix, son of Edouard, keeper of secrets, committer of crimes, target.

Felix, who, like me, played a part in a story he had not read.

*

Hospitals are horrible, generally. The Saint-Louis was different though, somehow warmer. Warmth can come from history. That morning, I felt more like I was entering a museum than an emergency ward. The Saint-Louis had been commissioned by Henry IV during the plague, when France's other hospitals were overflowing.

Some people find hospitals comforting. Many patients, given a choice to stay, will remain in the hospital as long as possible. The illusion of protection is a powerful placebo.

What would Marcus have said if we had had more time. What would we have done. Later, after everything was over, I would think often of the Komodo dragons on his dressing gown, what he said the morning of the wedding about defining happiness just for us. I believe he meant it. I believe he meant everything he ever said to me. I would think about our swim the morning of the wedding, about how he'd tasted the icing on his finger first before placing it in my mouth. Memory is less binary over time.

As I entered the hospital two men approached and indicated they were "with me" and would be leading me to the child. They were not the men from that day in the restaurant, which is to say not men I recognized as part of Raja's team, but they looked familiar. Had they been to the house at Cap Ferret before, I couldn't tell. As we passed down a long central hall, I glimpsed another man in a waiting area reading *Paris Match*. He wore a suit and a ball cap with the insignia of the Turkish football team Beşiktaş. When Marcus worked out, he often wore a Beşiktaş jersey. Simple white tennis shoes peeked out from under the man's impeccably tailored pants, and as I turned my head to look more closely, he glanced up and looked back.

We took the elevator to the top floor, the "privé" wing. The lighting was better there, gentler. The floor had elaborate carpeting as opposed to linoleum, and there were stylish, if anodyne, black-and-white photographs lining the walls. The French monuments—the Arc de Triomphe, the Eiffel Tower, the Louvre. In the final photograph before we reached large double doors at the end of the hall, there it was: the Musée Rodin.

Confidence, confidence, confidence.

I was learning to exhibit less emotion.

I was learning answers come to those who wait.

One of the men opened the door for me then closed it behind me, staying back in the hall. The room, enormous and blandly, elegantly furnished, like a hotel suite, was completely quiet. Canal+ Sport played on mute via an enormous flat screen TV along one wall. Tiny bottles of water were lined up on a bedside table along with a small bowl of red licorice. The patient, sound asleep, had a comic book folded across his chest, Astérix and Obélix. I could see clearly that it was the boy who had sat next to me at lunch at Cap Ferret, who had talked about sports. I stood awkwardly for a minute, mindful of what Raja had said about time, anxious as it did not look like this little boy would, or could, go anywhere soon, definitely not in twenty minutes. I watched him breathe and wondered what the problem was. I walked to the windows at the far side of the room and looked out over the tenth arrondissement.

A nurse entered the room.

"*Bonjour*," she said, then shifted to English. "He has his medicine now," she said and moved toward the boy, gently touching his shoulder. His eyes opened and she handed him two tiny pills and a glass of water. The boy looked at me.

"Hello there, you," he said.

"Hello," I said.

"Have you come to break me out of here," he asked, optimistically.

"Definitely not that," said the nurse. "You will be here for a while."

And, as if on cue, my two new friends entered from the hall and, while one packed the boy's things into a bag, the other rolled a wheelchair to the edge of the bed.

"*Merci, Max,*" said the boy, as if it were perfectly ordinary to pull rank against a nurse when you're the patient. To the other man he said simply, "*Ça va, Georges.*"

The men moved fast.

They were minding Raja's clock, too.

Georges told the nurse to bring him enough medication "*pour dix jours,*" but the nurse fought back, clearly unaware she was punching above her weight, unaware of the slim Glock pistols concealed in the men's trousers, weapons I would notice only later when they stepped up into the helicopter before me in order to pass Felix comfortably into his seat, in the process lifting a hem an inch too high. No, the nurse was doing what any fine nurse would do, advocating for the patient, *first, do no harm* and all that. As the argument escalated, the nurse blocked the door. And that was when the doctor arrived.

After apologizing profusely to Max and Georges, the doctor instructed the nurse to leave. He handed the men a small package tied with string and assured them that all they needed was inside, "three times a day, still water not sparkling, and lots of rest."

He bent down to Felix's eye level and took the boy's hands in his own.

"Do you know who I am," the doctor said.

Felix shook his head.

"Well, this is *my* hospital, and I know *everything* about all of my patients. Would you like to know what I know about you."

Felix nodded.

"I know that you are going to be completely fine. But you must take care of yourself. No football on the lawn, do you understand?"

Felix nodded.

The doctor reached into his pocket and pulled out a candy bar.

"Chocolate, daily, also essential."

The doctor glanced at me and retreated. From there all the way to the car and from the car all the way to the helicopter, Felix spoke to Max and Georges about sports. He spoke with them like they were brothers, not bodyguards. When we were at last in the air, the teddy bear on the seat between us, Felix turned to me and said, "I am so happy you're coming back. And my father will be happy, too."

"Your father?"

"*Oui,* my father, Edouard. He is so looking forward to seeing you."

"What else did he say?"

"He says you remind him of an old friend, from the war."

It would not be the last time I would hear that word, "war," but the only time I ever heard it spoken by a child. "War" is a word adults use often, casually, as a metaphor, *war on drugs, war on crime, warring lovers.* That day in the car I had the clear sense that for Felix, and for his father, war was not a metaphor at all. War was a precise, objective way to describe their lives.

VII

A COMPLICATED MAN

No one was waiting to greet us when we landed. Felix seemed relieved to be home. I wondered if and how I would learn more about what was wrong with him, or just how sick he was. I wondered what the next days would be like. He ran out under the blades and toward the house, as if flights home via helicopter were no big thing, as if he had done that run a thousand times, as if being in your pajamas after noon was perfectly acceptable. Felix had more confidence than I did, and I envied that. I wondered what, or whom, he was running toward.

The men took my bags and the teddy bear, and I started to walk the path I had walked before with Nikki, newly attuned to everything around me not only as it felt like it was the job now, but also because forcing my mind to focus on the task at hand kept it from wandering. Wandering away to Marcus and loss. And, further afield and less appropriately, to Raja. When I thought about Raja now, I had a new and increasingly obsessive need to know if he was thinking of me, too. If he ever thought of me outside the context of the work. On arriving back at the Cap I had learned a lot of things, but I hadn't yet understood that for Raja, everything was transactional. Even emotion. *Especially* emotion. What I was to Raja was a means to an end—not an end in and of itself. And an end of this game was something Raja desperately needed.

Dasha stood on the steps by the entrance.

She pulled me into her, as if she was the one who needed support.

As if she was the one who was suffering.

I expected her to say something about the hospital.

Instead, she said, "I was wrong about you." And, "I am so very sorry for your loss."

A housekeeper offered me a bottle of water then led me upstairs to a small library off of which was another bedroom, with a window from which you could see the sea. A writing desk, a chaise, and two small slipper chairs on top of which were folded, impeccably, several swimsuits, swimming caps, and towels. On the walls, two parallel lines of old master drawings, reproductions, stared down at me as if to remind me I was in a place of history, and taste. Marcus loved old masters. He used to say we would go to Italy one day and see "the best ones." Even though I had now introduced myself as fluent in the history of Italian art and could speak with relative ease about things like the loggia of the Villa San Michele and how far a drive it is from Milan to Cortina, I had never been to Italy. Many years later, when I finally saw Rome for the first time, it was like stepping into a past life. Tell a lie about yourself often enough and it becomes dangerously close to the truth. I looked in the mirror and told myself, *I am here to mourn the loss of* my husband. I said it out loud.

"I am here to mourn the loss."

I did not say, *I am not here to infiltrate this perfectly happy family, gain their trust, and then betray them.* I did not say, *you have absolutely no clue what you're doing.*

"This is the prettiest room," the maid said, in heavily French-accented English.

She was standing in the doorway. She'd brought my bags. She'd brought Max, too.

Max entered and placed the luggage on a wicker bench at the foot of the bed. The maid placed fresh flowers in small crystal vases on either side of the desk. On the desk, a perfectly square piece of light blue paper was printed with a meal schedule, as if this were camp. Camp, or the military. "Déjeuner" was at "quatorze heures," or two o'clock, an hour away. I removed the photograph of Marcus from my bag and set it on the bedside table. I looked at him, and wished he were there. I didn't care what his real name was. I didn't care what he had failed to tell me. I felt so sure that if he could talk to me at that moment, he would explain everything.

I lay on the bed and stared at the ceiling for a minute before I noticed a tiny dark dot in the ceiling's corner. It was just above the molding and not even the size of a dime.

"I don't have eyes inside this place, but I can assure you they have cameras everywhere," Jack had said, back at the hotel in Paris. I had taken a break to use the bathroom. I wasn't sure if he knew I could hear him through the door.

"You're paranoid," Annabel said.

"I'm *right*."

I looked at the dot and realized that dot might be looking back at me. And who else had lain in this bed and been watched, with or without their knowledge. That dot was the first clear indication that I wasn't the only one taking notes. Any spy can hide a camera in a pinhole if they like. That dot camera was designed to be noticed, as subtle as an armed guard patrolling the hall.

Lunch, like before, was outside under the pergola, but a light rain had apparently scared some people off. There was no Nikki, and the children were all eating inside, off the kitchen in a kind of playroom. Four adults sat at the far end of the long table, men in tracksuits speaking Russian. Which left Dasha and me to effectively eat alone. There were egg salad sandwiches and a thick, green cold soup. The grapes had been replaced with fresh figs, and the vases at each place that day held sprigs of mint, not flowers. I remember how Dasha took the mint and broke it into pieces into her iced tea, then encouraged me to do the same.

"It was a heart attack," she said, "your husband."

"He had heart disease," I said.

"How long were you married?"

"Six weeks." And she waited, and I didn't add anything, and she backed down.

"It really doesn't matter, does it," she said. "You can live with someone for decades and not love them at all."

"I am grateful for your kindness."

"Come and go as you please here. We are casual people."

"Thank you."

"And you will marry again, one day, I am sure of that."

"How is Felix," I said.

"Felix will be fine."

The rain began to come down harder. Five men in black slacks and T-shirts moved in around us to pull down plastic curtains from the pergola's roof, enclosing us in a clear tent and providing the illusion that we were inside the storm. And yet completely protected and dry. I remembered the photograph Jack had laid on the bed.

"Felix is my husband's son," she said, "as perhaps you know. Though I am young enough to have been his mum. He doesn't really want a mum. He only wants his father."

"Raja said," I started, and she interrupted me.

"What *did* Raja say."

"He said you were kind."

"Did he tell you why we live here?"

"No."

"Well, we came here because we didn't feel safe, anymore, in Beirut."

"Beirut?"

"Yes. Edouard's business is there. *Was* there. And Felix's mother had lived there. I never met her, but I hear she was rebellious, uncaged. Like my stepson, ordering around bodyguards to break out of hospital. Only a very spoiled child would do that, don't you think."

And because it felt like some kind of a test I simply said, "The doctor seemed to think that it was all right for him to leave."

"I can assure you the doctor was compensated for his flexibility."

The rain was letting up. The men at the other end of the table left plates piled with biscotti and rock candy behind and, as they passed us, looked at me, nodded to Dasha.

"*Spasibo. Spasibo. Spasibo,*" they said. *Thank you. Thank you. Thank you.*

Dasha said she was going to take a nap and asked me to join her, later, for a walk. We agreed to meet on the beach at six o'clock, but when I arrived at the beach wearing one of the swimsuits that had been placed, so lovingly, in my room, it wasn't Dasha waiting. It was Edouard. And I could see him clearly now, and he was not at all what I had imagined. He looked at me like we were old friends. And then he shook his head.

He was tall, six foot three or four at least, if I had to guess, gently towering over me as I approached. Slim, if not wiry. Raja had said he was sixty-three, but he looked younger. His blue linen shirt was unbuttoned to his chest, sleeves casually rolled up like a schoolboy. He wore swimming trunks embroidered with little sea turtles swimming in circles, navy on white. He looked like one of Marcus's bankers I had met by the pool in Mallorca, in the days leading up to the wedding. Always casually, yet precisely, pulled together. He moved like a dancer, not a soldier, as if I knew how soldiers moved. Raja had said that "from what we know" Edouard was sickly and weak. The belief was that he didn't leave the house, and that had been a problem. The belief was that he might be confined to his room. The belief with "high confidence" was that he had gained an enormous amount of weight, in part to disguise himself. The belief was that, in any event, he was no longer a direct threat to anyone, anymore.

None of this applied to the man before me.

He was like a movie star on holiday.

He did not look afraid. He did not look evil.

"Oh, 'evil' is a bit of a stretch, don't you think," Jack had said, pushing back on Raja's use of the word.

Jack had said that when he returned one final time to see me. It was just before the suitcases arrived. He claimed he had returned to "wish me luck," but coincidentally he'd arrived in my room at the exact moment Raja moved from the window to the bed. Raja had crossed his legs and when he did his foot touched my ankle. I remember Raja was looking at me when Jack knocked on the door. Had Jack been outside that hotel door all along. Was Jack waiting to enter at the exact moment when Raja looked at me with something like affection, and had Jack been instructed that that was the moment to knock on the door. I will never know. I assumed Jack had been looking for Raja, that there was something he wanted to discuss.

"You don't like the word 'evil' because you're *Catholic*," Raja had said.

"I am not only Catholic, I am *Irish*, so I actually *appreciate* the concept of evil. Central tenet of the worldview."

"I thought the central tenet was forgiveness," said Raja, and Jack laughed.

"Aleksey likes power. Any evil he accrues along the way is gravy."

"Who is Aleksey," I had said, but no one answered.

As I walked closer toward him on the beach, Edouard put out his hand.

"I am very sorry for your loss," he said.

"Thank you. It's very beautiful here."

"I was bored by city life. And now I cannot imagine living anywhere else."

He started to walk and gestured for me to follow.

"How did you and Dasha meet?"

"We were colleagues. And we missed the memo about mixing business with pleasure."

He pointed to a high cliff a mile ahead of us and suggested we walk there. He said that the view was "unreal" and that he would show me the way to the top. "If you're feeling ambitious." He said he liked getting his exercise each day now by climbing. He said he had never felt healthier, or younger, than he had living near the ocean. As we walked, he gave me a brief history of that part of France. And he told me that as a child his parents had taken him to Normandy one Christmas, "to see the beaches, the American cemetery, the German cemetery, so much loss" and how he knew then that one day he would live in this part of the world. "I like being close to the history," he said. "Close to the ghosts."

As we climbed slim stone steps carved, if roughly, into the

bluff, I could hear his breathing. I thought about how men never like to concede weakness, pain, or need. I thought about Jack's green eyes set like a hawk as he clocked Raja's foot glance my ankle. What did Jack think of me. Creative thinking was Jack's "comparative advantage," Raja had put it. Jack was "a *magician* at story," which was not unrelated to his success as a precise, innovative assassin. Jack could see "in three dimensions, around corners, through walls." Jack was an alien, too. Who else but an alien would choose that kind of work? Raja told me that Jack's nickname, earned after time spent attached to MI6, was "Freestyle." The Brits were wary of him at first, as they would be of most Irishmen, but they came to admire him above anyone else. "Freestyle" was a nod to the skiers who perform elaborate tricks at high speed and altitude, on a steep incline.

When we reached the top of the cliff Edouard led me to a small grassy area from which you could look west, out over the Atlantic, with pristine blue ocean and azure sky forever, marred only by the occasional gull. The gulls, like the jet skis, circled as if with a will to watch over us.

"What did you think of my paintings," he asked, eventually.

His gold watch was not set to local time.

"I have never seen anything like them," I said.

It was a relief to say something true.

"Have you ever read the *Iliad*," he asked.

I hadn't, and so he told me the story.

He told me about Helen and Paris. About Homer's choice of language, how he led with, "the *rage* of" Achilles. As the sun dropped in the sky he told me about Achilles's love for Patroclus, his close friend, and about how after Hector, the son of Priam and enemy of Achilles, brutally killed Patroclus in the war, Achilles killed Hector in revenge. And he told me how Priam snuck into Achilles's camp at night and at great personal risk.

"He confronted his son's assassin," Edouard said. "Imagine what that would feel like."

"Did he kill Achilles?"

"No, no he was a very old man. He was too weak to kill the brave, young warrior. What Priam wanted was the body of his son. He wanted to give his son a proper burial. And I've always believed he wanted a level of atonement, too."

"Atonement for what."

"For his son's sins, his own sins, the sins of the war. Priam knew he and Achilles shared in the slaughter, in different ways. It is in finding what we share that we find grace."

"And does Achilles agree."

"He does."

It was getting colder.

It never once occurred to me, on that walk, that I might be in danger.

I can only describe Edouard's behavior that night as gentle.

"What happens in the end?" I asked.

"Priam wept for his child, and Achilles wept for his friend, and Achilles agreed to stand down his army and allow Priam to bury Hector in peace. What most readers don't remember is the *Iliad* does not end with war. It ends with women. With the burial. With Hector's grief. And that is what I had hoped my paintings might convey."

He led me across the ridge to its far edge to reveal, a foot below, a flat, square shelf, pointing north over the water. It almost looked like it might have been an accident of ancient weather, a breaking off of rock leaving this one piece suspended above the sea. In fact, it was the skilled work of a local craftsman who had managed not only to meld the flat rock onto the cliffside but to secure it in such a way that it could bear the weight of several people. It was perfectly smooth, a jewel soldered to the edge of a giant frame. At the center of this little landing, a small white stone cross was set into a round O of bright green moss. It was a gravesite.

"*The Iliad* acknowledges war as essential to human life. It presents violence without sentiment," Edouard said, looking at the cross. "Homer was Greek, but the *Iliad* is a very Russian story. Any Russian understands these concepts."

"Who is buried here," I said.

And after a very long time he said, "Me, one day. This is my gravesite."

The wind was coming up. Edouard put his arm around me in an explicitly paternal way and thanked me for helping "my Felix, who probably has a crush on you now; he likes older women." He said he hoped I would stay as long as I liked. He added, "Dasha needs company. And Nikki does, too, though she'd never admit it." And then, almost as an afterthought, he added that the only rule of the place, which perhaps I had already guessed, was discretion.

"We are private people," he said.

"I understand."

*

On entering the house Edouard stopped in the foyer and looked around, almost as if he were lost. The dogs slept peacefully in a corner. I waited, as if I needed his permission to move. I waited for him to say that he could see through me, through the swimsuit and the new hair and all the acquired attitude, through the fake knowledge and barely-there self-possession, through my entire life back to my childhood. He was looking at me and saying nothing, and I remembered my mother's brothers forcing me to make them laugh. I had always been performing for someone.

"I am not going to sell them," he said.

He said that he had decided to give the paintings, one day, to a museum, where "another generation" could contemplate "all the things you and I talked about tonight." He asked what I thought about that. And I thought about where those paintings might sit, somewhere between the *Mona Lisa* and the *Winged Victory,* about how even though I wasn't a scholar, I knew enough to understand how almost all of art history can be confined to a few major categories.

"That's very generous," I said.

"Why don't we walk again, tomorrow." And just like that, a pattern was set.

He turned and walked across the room to the door leading to the stairs.

No one at the Cap ever said goodbye.

Everyone there seemed to live in an eternal present.

A world walled off from consequence.

Over the next days I would learn a lot about Edouard's interests. They included, in addition to art and history, revenge, loss, empathy. And, maybe above all, human error. I would learn, during those days, that Edouard's views of the world were vastly different from mine, informed by a complex personal history, and by his service. All my old ideas about the world started to erode after that first walk with Edouard. My ignorant, youthful confidence was receding, a wave soon to be replaced by something new. I was learning. I would learn that Edouard's entire life had been defined by things that had happened long before we met, things

not taught in classrooms or written into history books. Edouard
saw everything differently. His intelligence was exhilarating to be
around, even though he was never boastful or sharp with it.

*

For the next nine nights, and always before dinner, Edouard and
I would walk the beach, climb the stone stairs, and stand at the
edge of the cliff as the sun set. He would always do most of the
talking, mainly telling me stories of Russian history, or of France.
He loved Greek myths. He told me about his family and how his
mother was known as one of the finest cooks in Moscow, how
she left when he was a boy and how his father raised him accom-
panied by the "unique tyranny" of three older brothers. On the
night of what would turn out to be our last walk I remember
falling asleep thinking perhaps I would stay at the Cap forever,
that perhaps the real dream was not this place but all the things
that had come before it, that maybe *this* was my new family and
home. There, for a brief time, I felt happy. And increasingly I
understood, these are good people. These people are not capable
of hurting anyone.

*

On my fifth day there I woke up with a strange mix of hunger
and nausea, something I had never experienced before. Within
an hour I was on the bathroom floor, wrapped in a towel, wondering if whatever this was would all end in some small, coastal
French emergency room. A shooting pain in my abdomen gave
way, eventually, to a low chronic cramp. I remember hearing the
children outside. The children played tag on their break from

the home school Dasha ran every day except Sundays from eight until three, after which they swam in the pool then retreated to bedrooms for naps before snacks, then it was time for exercise, before evening baths and supper. Everything in their lives was highly organized, the casual element that had defined my first visit revealed as an aberration. On most days, everyone had precisely scripted schedules. Everyone, except Edouard.

Edouard didn't eat with the rest of us, and though we would meet for our walks, I rarely saw him otherwise. And during the entire time I spent there I never saw him touch Dasha once. They acted like colleagues, not lovers, treating each other with a kind of cool respect and efficiency. It never occurred to me to doubt, like Annabel, that they had been in love, once. With me, Edouard was different. He was, with me, more like he was the times I saw him interact with Felix. Protective, expansive, funny. With Dasha, there were no jokes and no stories. With Dasha, there were logistics. Dasha never questioned our evenings walks.

On cold days, as on the day I had arrived, the children ate lunch separately off the kitchen, in a small glasshouse lined with boxwoods. Three cages at the far end held bunny rabbits, for play, as opposed to the large lapins the cook ordered biweekly for stews. Three teachers arrived each morning from a school in the nearest town, ferried by black SUVs commandeered by Georges's men. I learned Georges "ran point on the detail," that Georges was, after Dasha, in charge. The cook told me that the day Georges had learned I was there to "process loss" he no longer saw me as a potential threat. A second, elite, and almost entirely invisible detail secured the compound. You rarely saw them, they were too discreet. I learned that the subjects for "school" included English, French, Russian, history, mathematics, science, and art. How each day would end with a "reading" of a classic work of literature or, on occasion, the Bible. Prayers were said before meals, and at bedtime and then the children, all in one way or another related to either Edouard or Dasha via cousins or nieces and nephews seemed to have no sense of the strangeness, the insularity, of their lives. I was told that most of the children came for a week then left. Only Felix remained. Felix, who seemed perennially nonplussed. Often, in the early evening, I would see him in the little greenhouse listening to sports on a small portable radio.

A child doesn't know what denial is.

A child loves fairy tales as the horror takes place at safe remove.

Any nine-year-old knows a house cannot be made of gingerbread.

Any nine-year-old knows a wolf doesn't talk.

Felix was right back to his studies the day after our return from Paris. He seemed, to me, fine. I remember looking around and wondering if, one day, all of this would be his. And whether he would even want it. I thought about how, when Felix was older, our age difference wouldn't matter so much; we were barely more than a decade apart. In many ways, he acted older than I did. He acted like he had seen it all, and yet was never condescending. Only later did I understand that was his finest defense. Felix never let you know what he was really thinking, a trick he'd no doubt learned along the way. His entire life, I would learn, was defined by running away from something. And, far more powerfully, by creating an idea of who his father was in order to defend himself against the truth.

*

"Jesus, are you all *right.*"

It was Nikki, standing at my bathroom door. She was eating

from a small plate with toast, butter, and jam, probably meant for me, which was just like her. She took casual ownership of everything around her, even people.

"I am fine," I said, moving a hand over my hip bone.

She sat down on the floor next to me and crossed her legs.

"You don't look fine," she said, more like a therapist than a physician. "Where does it hurt?"

"Here. And here. And here."

"When was your last period."

"I don't remember."

"Well, you're probably pregnant," she said, like she was reading the weather.

I assured her I simply needed rest.

"Well, please stop resting soon as I leave after lunch."

"Leave?"

"Yes, real life calls, at long last."

"Where is real life?"

"Ah, now, that's a *very* good question."

And she placed the plate on the floor beside me and left.

Real life, I thought, is a place without graves for the living.

Real life doesn't have cameras embedded in the walls.

Real life has no pseudonyms, cover stories, or elegant exfiltration plans.

I stood up and looked in the mirror. *This is my real life.*

"I'll be back for the party," Nikki said, alerting me to the fact that she hadn't left the bedroom. Had she been spying on me? Did she think I was pretending? I looked into the mirror, and there she was behind me.

"What party," I said.

"Edouard's birthday. He probably won't come, but Dasha's planned it."

"Why do you call your mother Dasha."

"I don't know. What do you call *your* mother."

She poked her head around the bathroom door. She licked jam off her palm.

"He's a Cancer, Edouard. His zodiac sign. You know what Cancer means, don't you," she said.

"No."

"Cold, remote, dangerous."

"Sounds like an iceberg."

"Ha, yes."

And I thought about the white cross, and the green moss, and Edouard's hand brushing my wrist.

Achilles and Priam in the tent, what Edouard had told me about how, when Hector put his battle helmet on, he'd frightened his son. The boy could not recognize his father when his father had his armor on. Perhaps that was why Edouard always seemed disarmed around me, and around Felix. I could not imagine Edouard threatening anyone, ever, at all.

"The iceberg likes you," she said, as if it were a warning.

After Nikki left, I opened a drawer under the sink and removed the small terry makeup case. Inside was the phone from Raja. I opened it. There were two "apps" on the home screen: ADDRESS BOOK and CALCULATOR. I opened the former and found two numbers: HOME and FREELANCE. Raja and Jack. I pressed FREELANCE and waited while it rang once, twice, three times. On the fifth ring someone picked up. It wasn't Jack.

"Ilium," said a woman's voice I didn't recognize, with unemotional efficiency.

Another wave of intense, acute nausea shot up from my waist straight to my brain.

"Who is speaking," the woman said.

"I am looking for Jack," I said.

And the line went dead.

*

The last time Marcus and I had sex was on the boat, before Paris. He had seemed so completely alive and present, not at all like a man who would be dead soon. Though he had told me that a heart problem had left him at acute risk of a stroke, and that the medications he had been taking were now contraindicated with another, older, health issue about which he was vague, I didn't believe it at all. Marcus was going to live forever, is what I believed. We would go on just like this. I was clear on that. In fact, he had to live forever, we still had so much to do. We had to define our happiness. We had to finish the garden. We had to have a child. Above all, we had to have a child so that it would all feel real.

A child may know that a house can't be built of gingerbread, but a woman in love will believe anything. Marcus knew that, and Raja knew it, too. I was the perfect choice for them, less for being an orphan, for being unsophisticated, and for being needy, than for wanting a story in which to believe. Wanting to be loved.

Marcus's then new, intense desire to have a baby didn't track with a man facing death. Why would anyone do that to the woman they love. Why would they do that to a child? Everything about that night in Dubrovnik was perfect, though. The precision of Marcus's toe tapping mine, playfully, on the deck. How he pulled me into him as the water got rough. How he never judged if, for example, my hair wasn't brushed or my shoes were dirty. My flaws seemed to amuse him. That night before Paris it was all laid out in front of us. Later that night would represent something else entirely. A final chapter in the story of the girl I once was.

The phone buzzed.

UNKNOWN NUMBER.

I picked it up. "Hello."

"Well, I thought you'd *never* call," Jack said.

"I think I need a pregnancy test."

"Ah. Congratulations," he said, drawing the five syllables out ominously. "Give us a few hours."

And the line went dead again.

I stayed in my room all that morning until someone knocked on the door and said, "*Déjeuner.*" The nausea had subsided. I dressed then walked down and out to the pergola, where Dasha sat in her usual chair, a space next to her empty, now our norm, for me. On her other side I was pleasantly surprised to see Felix, who hadn't taken a meal with us since we had gotten back from the Saint-Louis. I sat down and he immediately explained, "I told my father I wanted to have lunch with the grown-ups today. The grown-ups have better desserts."

We ate freshly cubed melon and sliced cold steak. The ripe grapes were now back on the table, obediently in their line. Enormous pitchers of variously flavored iced teas were passed, and the men in their tracksuits were smoking before the first course was over. It occurred to me that those men might not be guests. Maybe they worked for Edouard or had, once. Maybe they were not on holiday but in hiding. No one ever introduced them or told me their stories. Felix talked about his latest math lessons and how he had decided he liked math because "everything is clear. There is, or is not, a right answer. It's like sports. There is, or is not, a clear winner. There is no problem you cannot solve, if you have the right methods."

Dasha stepped away to take a phone call. When the plates were being cleared and the other guests stood to leave, Felix asked if he could "visit me later," and I said I would like that very much. As I was about to leave, Nikki arrived and said to Felix, "I need a moment alone with my friend."

"She's *my* friend, too," said Felix.

As if it was a competition.

As if there was a right answer.

"Of course she is."

And Felix, feeling like the winner, went off to join his class.

Nikki handed me a small brown paper parcel wrapped in string, which I opened to find a pregnancy test. I looked at her and she mouthed the words, *"De rien," you're welcome.* Had she been listening to my call to Jack, or was it possible that Nikki knew Jack? Was Nikki part of the team, Raja's inside man, and if she was, did that mean I was not alone. Or maybe Nikki was there to keep track of me to make sure I didn't go off script, a kind of minder.

"I don't want you to leave," I said, and I meant it, whoever she was. Her presence was a buffer for me against what was starting to feel like an unwanted intimacy from Edouard, potential conflict with Dasha—and who knows what would happen to my relationship with Felix. If I was pregnant, I would need a friend.

"Change of plan," she said, and pulled me into a hug.

I went back to my room and lay on the bed, staring up at the dot. I didn't want to take the test but knew I had to. As I started to do the math, speaking of, in my mind of what a baby in my life might mean I never once considered that I would not want to keep it, him, her. I did think about how Marcus was so focused and intent on my getting pregnant. As I thought back through every time we had talked about a baby, I suddenly saw it differently. What if, in Marcus's view, my having a baby was not selfish. It was a gift, a sign of his love. A baby would afford me a way out of the situation into which Marcus, and Raja, had placed me.

It never occurred to me to look at the baby another way.

That the arrival of a baby might not free me at all but rather deepen, and solder, my dependence.

I took the test.

And I waited.

And then there they were, the two thin blue lines.

I was going to have a baby.

"Tut, tut, it looks like rain," someone said, from the other side of the bathroom door. Felix.

"Just a minute," I said.

"Come swimming," he said, and I could see through the window that clouds were gathering.

I suddenly worried that if I went out with Felix now I wouldn't get my evening walk with Edouard.

I opened the door. Felix was standing there wearing enormous swim goggles pushed up on his forehead. He held a second set in his hand and held them out to me.

"We can snorkel. There are not many fish but it's fun. I will take you to the Dune, too."

"All right, that will be fun."

Instead of walking to the beach off the house, Felix, who had waited patiently for me in the hall, walked me to the front door and out to a waiting car, where the ever-runic Georges was waiting. I wondered if Georges had access to the cameras in my room and if he sat up late at night, eating leftovers, watching me sleep. *In the hotel of decisions, the guests sleep well.* What did that mean.

I never saw Georges eat, not once. I never noticed him express an emotion. I trust he took pains to be invisible but, to me, that only increased my desire to know who he was, by which story he had come here, and what secrets he kept. Who did Georges believe he was serving, and at what cost?

"It's a bit of a drive," said Felix, "but we won't be *too* long."

"What about school?"

"Papa said I could miss it."

"And why is that."

"Well, he said you won't be here forever, and that I should take you to see something new. I think he's worried you're bored with us."

"That's very kind of him."

"And, he rarely says no to me."

I wondered if, one day, when I had a child Felix's age, I would be unable to say no to her, or him, too. Despite being at clear risk of being spoiled, Felix was so open and kind, so entirely self-possessed, his manners so far advanced for his age. A child with advanced manners can be a freak, or a moving example of a certain denied innocence. Felix often did things I don't associate with children. He stood back so that I could get into the car first. He offered me the bottle of water Georges had handed to him. And what I remember most from those days was how Felix always asked what I was thinking, a very adult kind of question. And how I was feeling, a question even most adults rarely care to ask. And Felix seemed genuinely to care about my answers. That preternatural, empathic curiosity was his defining trait. I observed him playing at being normal, trying to hew to rituals that ordinary children participate in, rituals he must have learned from television shows. A part of him wanted to be normal, like any child, and perhaps not acknowledge his very unordinary environment. Most children aren't homeschooled in pristine compounds staffed by bodyguards carrying AK-47s. If we had had more time and I had had more courage, I would have asked Felix how *he* felt, what *he* was thinking. It had never occurred to me, not once, that Felix might be part of the plan.

We drove for almost thirty minutes without saying anything. I wanted to open my phone and Google "I'm pregnant, now what," but Felix's presence provided a defense against that. When Georges turned off the two-lane main road onto a sandy side street, Felix's excitement was visible, and in that I could finally glimpse the little boy inside. As if we were approaching the Christmas tree on Christmas morning. As if the next turn toward the beach would reveal some spectacular surprise. A go-cart, a pony, a bouncy house.

"This is the best surf break on the Cap," he said, as the turn revealed simply another long stretch of beach. "Some surfers think it's the best in all of Western Europe, excepting Spain, but France is so much prettier than Spain, don't you think? My father used to like to come and watch the surfers, when we first arrived. He says their patience calms him."

"Why doesn't he watch them anymore?"

"I don't know."

Georges parked the car. He opened my door and handed me two enormous beach towels emblazoned with the French flag. As I took them from him, he held on a split second too long. Looking at me, Georges promised he would be waiting, that we should take our time, and motioned to a picnic basket in the trunk, running me through a list of its contents. Felix wasn't listening.

Felix wasn't hungry. Felix had moved away from the car and was motioning for me to follow him through a grove of small trees and down a rocky path onto the widest beach I had ever seen. It was empty. Out in the water, though, I could see them before Felix pointed, the surfers. The wind was low that day so they were sitting, or lying, on their boards. The patience Edouard admired.

"Sometimes they sit there for hours," Felix said.

"Do you think they get bored."

"No. They know it's simply a matter of time."

He threaded a bright blue snorkel through a loop in his goggles' side then handed another one to me.

His enormous eyes.

He seemed never to blink.

"Wot," he said, staring at me through the plastic. He had caught my smile.

"Well, the idea that anything is simply 'a matter of time' is just a very grown-up idea."

"I am way more grown up than you think," he said, less a challenge than a kind of confession.

And, in that moment, I thought about his mother and wondered how she had died and how much Felix knew about her, about his father and his stepmother, about why they were living there and how long it would last. Felix walked ahead of me and, with the fearlessness only children possess, dove into a high breaking wave. And then he was gone, and I couldn't see him, and so I raced into the water and dove in, too.

"Pretty spectacular, right?" Felix said, after our swim and another short drive to the Dune. We'd dried off and Felix had eaten a chocolate bar taken from a candy cache in the car's glove compartment. The car, like the compound, had everything for everyone, it seemed. "Georgie is a sugar addict," Felix had said, but

Georges, strange Georges, Georges who was undoubtedly trained to kill me at close range if he liked, Georges who'd held the towels a split second too long in what felt like a sign. Georges said nothing. It was clear the candy existed exclusively for Felix. Haribo, Smarties, also his American favorites, Sugar Daddies and MilkyWays. "My father likes licorice, and only on special occasions, otherwise he barely eats sugar at *all*," Felix said. "Isn't that horrible."

We walked over the Dune until the weather started to turn.

It must have been close to six.

I didn't have my phone. I didn't wear a watch.

"I think I need to get back," I said.

"Why," he asked.

"I promised your father I would walk with him," I said, and seeing his face fall, I wondered if this was not simply the latest in a long line of disappointments Felix worked hard to hide. On our ride back he barely spoke, and when we pulled onto the gravel circle at the side of the house, he left the goggles and snorkel on his seat and went soundlessly inside. As if I had rejected him. Which, in a way, I had.

"Don't worry," said Georges, apparently human after all.

"I think I disappointed him," I said.

"He is used to disappointments."

And, as if he had said too much, Georges lowered his sunglasses and got out of the car, leaving me alone in the back.

In the hallway, Edouard waited, reading the *Financial Times*. He folded the paper on his lap as I entered.

"I fear I have stolen you from another man," he said. "And a very charming one, too."

I told him I had to go to my room quickly and he said to take my time, that dinner would be late that evening, or even delivered to rooms as a storm was coming. And people were tired, "it was a long day at work for all of us," as if that made sense to me. The nod to "work" was my first and fleeting confirmation of a suspicion gradually creeping toward confirmation, keyed initially off of Raja's stories and Jack's sly paranoia. A confirmation that Cap Ferret was not a home of holiday, that in fact things were happening here among the adults with a rigor and precision that paralleled the children's studies of Aristotle and algebra. The idea that something was being "worked on," and that perhaps the true nature of this work was the real thing I had been sent here to discover, and report back.

In the bathroom, I brushed my hair. I put on lipstick, mascara, and blush, like I was preparing for a date. Or as if I felt anyone who looked too closely could see the truth. As if Edouard's eyes were an ultrasound and could see right inside me, see exactly how many weeks away the life inside me was from being born. Perhaps see into my child's future. And, in seeing that, have some shot at controlling it.

I opened the drawer and the terry cloth makeup case, inside of which I had hidden the test as well as the box it came in. I should tear this to pieces and flush it down the toilet, that seemed like a sensible, secure choice, but when I tore off the cover, I noticed something affixed to its inside by a slim, almost invisible, strip of double-sided tape. I peeled it off, mindful Edouard was waiting, and opened the small piece of paper. It was no larger than a gum sweet wrapper. Someone had written three letters there in clear, black ink: **[D O B]**.

The newspaper was folded on the chair when I reentered the foyer, the dogs alert by the door. I could see Edouard through the screen, looking west toward the beach. He was wearing sunglasses and one more of the same linen shirt, always buttoned one button past halfway and sleeves always rolled precisely to the elbow.

Shirt always carefully untucked. This was Edouard's uniform. A uniform for a deployment, the goal of which, I would understand soon, was, like the silk map Annabel had laid out on my bed in Paris, "escape and evasion."

I stepped onto the porch and apologized for the delay.

"You're very beautiful," he said, and then started off on the walk.

He always set the pace.

As we were walking later than usual it was darker, the water rougher. We made it to the steps and up to the top of the bluff where the wind was now coming in hard. If those surfers were still waiting, they would have their breaks now.

"Did you see the surfers," Edouard asked.

"We did."

"They surf at night, too. Surfing at night is a form of Russian roulette."

He told me he learned to surf as a boy.

"It looks so effortless, but it is in fact a complex, dangerous business, at the highest levels."

He told me about the myth of the "hundred-foot wave" which turned out not to be a myth at all but rather the result of aberrant weather patterns and a deep cavity off of Nazaré, Portugal.

"Here, there is no break," he said, indicating the ocean. "There is no protection."

That night, Edouard didn't ask anything about me until we were almost at the house. The weather had turned rapidly, as he had predicted, and a light rain was already coming down. Up the stairs, on the porch now lit by a long line of glass lanterns arranged at perfect intervals along the floor, and hundreds of votives precariously placed atop the rail, Edouard took my arm. He used the slightest bit of force, as if guarding me against a fall.

"I would like you to stay longer," he said.

"Oh, I don't know," I said.

"Dasha has planned a party."

And it felt like ten minutes passed before he added, "Do you like parties."

"Parties are all right," I said, silently counting the number of parties I had attended in my entire life. It wasn't a long list.

"You can help with Felix."

"All right," I said.

All you have to do is listen.

Listen, and keep moving forward, like a shark.

There was no other choice.

This, it occurred to me, was the reason I was here.

I was here to draw Edouard out of hiding.

I looked up, half expecting to see Jack circling above with some strange surveillance device.

Had he been watching me all this time?

And could he see what I was feeling now.

The truth was, my days there *had* started to heal something in me.

As Edouard looked at me, I made a promise to myself. I would never forget those days. I would never forget the trip to the Dune and the candy in the glove compartment. How these people had treated me like I was a part of something. How they had treated me with dignity and respect. Could I say the same for Jack and Jill, for Annabel?

"You remind me of someone," Edouard said.

I could see movement inside the house behind him and wondered what Dasha was doing. At this hour she was probably running a bath, probably wondering what my time with Felix had been like. Perhaps she was feeling guilty for the days she had not spent with him. Motherhood is dynamic but stepmotherhood is consistent, oscillating between silence and exile. You think risk is navigating traffic with your eyes closed, try raising a child who is not your own. Dasha, I was certain, had had her rough nights. What kept her at the Cap, I always believed, was something other than the children.

Edouard took a step closer.

His shirtsleeves had unrolled down to his wrists.

The hem of his shorts was lined with sand.

In that moment he was neither immaculate nor impenetrable.

He was human.

What if everything I had been told about him was a lie.

"Tell me about her," I said.

"She was a surgeon."

"She must have been very smart."

"Oh, she was. And very beautiful. She saved my life, more than once."

"Did she operate on you?"

He stepped closer.

Someone called from inside, instructions to shut the windows. The storm was rising.

"No."

And closer.

"And where is she now."

"She's dead."

The moonlight, as it hits the white cross, is blinding.

As Priam entered Achilles's tent, he slowly removed his hood to reveal his eyes.

When you crest the wave at Nazaré, you lose your breath.

Edouard looked at me one last time then turned and walked

inside, the dogs falling in line on either side of him. I watched until he was entirely out of sight.

*

I was thinking about Felix and the chocolate bar when I opened the door to my room to find him sitting on my bed, in his pajamas, as if he did that every night, as if anything anymore was remotely normal.

"Hi," I said.

"Hi, you," he said, and raised an eyebrow.

I pulled the chair from the desk over to the bed and sat down. Felix's feet dangled more than a foot above the floor, a fact that made him seem even younger than he was. Nine. When I tried to remember what nine felt like all I could recall were arguments, brutal, violent "conversations" my parents would have almost daily, at almost the exact same hour, which is to say once they had each had a few drinks. Always after I had gone to bed but before I had fallen asleep, an accident or perhaps a choice of time, which, in retrospect, was particularly sadistic. Those arguments ensured I slept less and likely ensured the nightmares, too. I would listen and, at first, try to discern what they were saying, force a focus on the content as a way to press emotions down into that place of denial for which I was building up early architecture. People say couples who stay together for a long time end up having only one argument, the same argument, over and over and over. The best temperature for the bedroom at night. That slightly too flirtatious colleague. A child who misbehaves. Money. Money was the argument my parents had over and over, money being the one thing they craved, lacked, or if they had it fleetingly, immediately squandered. There might have been, here and there, money for a new dress. Or a sporty bicycle that my father could ride to the office and that made him feel young. Then my father would lose another newly acquired job due to his "rage" and come home to tell my mother that new dress would have to go back. My parents engaged in behavior far more ferocious than anything I had seen from Marcus, Raja, Jack or Jill, or Annabel or Edouard. If I had in fact entered into a world of a certain kind of warrior, it was far calmer and more civil than that of my childhood. Once, my father threw a plate at my mother. After it shattered, she had gathered the pieces and arranged them, neatly, on her bedside, as if they were a gift. As if she collected them.

Pieces of what.

Pieces of you.

Almost all of the "things" I remember from my childhood were "lost," taken away, recycled. Once, right around my ninth birthday, the party having been canceled at the last minute, my mother packed her bags and left. My father came home that night to find me sitting on his bed, my legs dangling above the floor. He had forgotten the birthday. It felt as if he had forgotten me, too. And even when my mother returned and begged his forgiveness, promising never to leave again, he didn't believe her. For a time, after that episode, there were home-cooked meals and nights of any television I wanted. There was baked Alaska and pancakes, and I remember tennis lessons and a visit to the zoo. Yes, wherever my mother had gone when she had left there had been money, and she had brought it back with her, using it to smooth my father's "rough edges," using it to please me. The money ended the evening arguments. And the money provided for more than one new dress and, for a few nights, my father had read to me before bed from a new set of books with fake-gold bindings. And then one day it all ended. Our little armistice broken by my mother's brothers bursting through the front door to drag my father into the yard. That was my first experience of violence.

"I am sorry," Felix said, and held out his hand to shake mine, like an investor or a politician. A little part of my heart broke, thinking someone must have taught him the value of a proper handshake.

"We had a lovely time," I said.

"I was *grumpy*," he said, and laughed.

"Well, we all get grumpy."

"Not my father, he is never grumpy."

"I don't know your father well enough to say, but I'll take your word for it."

"I have a very good word," he said. And then, "My father is a very busy man."

"I don't know what your father does," I said, gently, imperceptibly prying.

"He's a writer."

And with that Felix leapt off the bed, slid a few inches across the wood floor in his slippers, and walked to the desk.

"What does he write?"

"He makes up stories."

"What kinds of stories?"

"Stories for grown-ups."

"No fairy tales?"

"Oh, I think grown-ups like a good fairy tale."

It was hard to believe he was nine.

"That's true."

He turned around and looked at me.

"Will you be staying for the party?"

"If Dasha likes."

"It only matters what my father likes," he said. "And my father likes to please me, and I would like very much if you would stay."

And that settled it.

I would stay for the party.

Felix was at the door, the door was open and Felix almost on the other side of it when he asked one last question. "When is *your* birthday?" And even as I was finding the words—*the sixth of October*—I was remembering those three letters, D O B, and suddenly I understood. If DOB meant "date of birth," was the note a sign to be mindful about Edouard's birthday. Was it a signal to pay attention to what was to come. I didn't answer, and Felix was gone. I looked on the bed and could see he'd left something behind. A chocolate bar.

Within minutes there was a knock on my door. I expected Felix was back for his candy but when I opened it no one was there. A blue lacquered tray lay on the floor in the hall. On it, a bowl of pasta, some grilled fish, and a plate of vegetables. A carafe of wine, salt, pepper, flowers. And a note: "Please call if you need anything. Mind the storm. Dasha."

After dinner I checked my phone, which was plugged into an outlet by the sink, and noticed a missed call from UNKNOWN. I dialed Raja's number, let it ring three times, and was about to hang up when he answered.

"*Allô.*" He sounded very far away. "*Ça va?*"

"Oui, yes."

"Be sure to rest."

"There is the party coming."

And after only the briefest pause he said what anyone might say to that.

"Well, you will need a gift, for the host."

And the line clicked.

The storm was rising. Rain had pooled on the floor by the window.

I lifted my shirt up in front of the bathroom mirror.

I ran my hand over my abdomen.

I looked the same but felt different.

I was the same but was different.

A baby would require changes.

And now I had decisions to make.

VIII

WHAT IS DONE CANNOT BE UNDONE

The next morning, the weather had cleared and I wandered down to the pool to swim. The water was cool from the rain, and it felt good to move. I knew that by the time I returned to my room the bed would be made and the dinner tray removed, new towels placed in the bathroom. It was just like that there, all systems in place at all times. Nikki told me a story about a young couple who'd visited the month before who, upon arriving, had thrown their things all over their room, leaving a chaos of clothes and an unmade bed. "Also they hadn't even properly shut the shower off," when they left for dinner. After dessert, Dasha told the assembled guests she wanted to take everyone on a house tour. And so the young couple panicked, worried their room would raise Dasha's temper, but when the tour came to their door and Dasha opened it, everything was perfect. The clothes folded neatly on the bed. The bed made and turned down, suitcases stowed in a corner. The young couple was relieved. The tour continued, and everyone went to the porch for coffee. It was only later that night, when the couple finally went up to their bedroom to sleep, that they opened the door to find their chaos meticulously re-created, down to the pillow they'd thrown to the left of the window, the shower ominously running. The story is emblematic of Dasha. Dasha never let you forget she knew who you were, even if she participated in an attempt to hide it. Dasha made you your best you, but she could un-make you with a blink. The story made me wonder what, if any, adjustments Dasha had made for and to Edouard over their years together. And whether those adjustments were the real reason he stayed with her.

Coming up for air at the end of a lap to wipe my eyes, I saw Dasha sitting on one of the sun chairs. She was smoking. No one smoked anymore, then, and I hadn't ever seen Dasha smoke. Smoking, then, could be easily interpreted as self-destructive.

"Good morning," I said.

"We were *so* lucky to have that rain, we needed it."

In her left hand she held a tiny seashell, her ashtray.

"Edouard told me you have decided to stay, and join us for the birthday?"

"If that's all right with you."

And she just looked at me, as if we both knew it didn't matter.

I got out of the pool and dried off.

You are going to be a mother, I said to myself. *So grow up. All you have to do is listen.*

I lay down on the chair next to her.

"And where will you go, when you do leave."

Polite conversation was not in Dasha's wheelhouse; she was awkward at it.

"I think back to London."

Confidence, confidence, confidence.

"London is not what it once was," she said. "And so expensive."

She put her cigarette out.

I turned to look at her. I could have told the truth then as easily as a lie. I could have said what I wanted to say, that she had no idea what "London" was, or could be, for someone like me. That "expensive" was a word that meant one thing to her and another, entirely different thing to me. What I wanted to say was that her casual access to privilege, security, and beauty had spoiled her, that she had no idea what it meant to be trapped, hungry, alone. That she had no idea what it felt like to stand outside the garden. Said another way, I wanted to train all of my rage and misplaced emotion on Dasha, blame her in the absence of anyone else to blame. I was irrational. Of course I was. I was pregnant. Everything inside was moving at a speed I could not control.

Instead I simply said, "I will never be able to thank you for this time."

And I meant it, every single word.

"When I met Edouard," she said, "Nikki needed stability, protection. Edouard provided that."

"What happened to her father?"

"He died in the wars."

"Which wars."

"Edouard is loyal to people he loves. It's how he was raised. His father was a general, too. His father was strict, not very loving."

She lit another cigarette. And I let her talk.

"Edouard would prefer to be living in Ancient Rome, provided he could be emperor. Or perhaps Napoleonic times."

"Provided he could be Napoleon," I offered.

"Oh no, dear, Russians *despise* Napoleon."

I could see Nikki coming down the hill from the house toward us.

"You don't know anything about art, do you?" Dasha said.

Nikki could see me looking at her. She raised her hands above her head, a little dance, or cheer. Nikki lived in the chronic process of seducing everyone she'd ever met. She wore a bikini like a police officer wears a badge.

"Raja didn't send you here to see the paintings. If Edouard wants to sell something, he doesn't need help from a pretty young girl."

Nikki was coming through the apple trees at the far side of the pool. She reached up and plucked an apple from a branch. She broke the apple open into two halves with her bare hands. She twisted the stem off and threw it on the ground. She looked at me.

"Pretty girls are for other things," Dasha said. She was sending me back to my bedroom, allowing me to open the door to my meticulously reconstructed mess. She was telling me that she'd been cleaning up for me since I arrived. And she was placing me on notice, her services would shortly expire.

"At the start of any war everyone believes they're on the right side," Dasha said, just as Nikki walked up to us, her hand held out with half the apple, an offering.

She kissed us each and sat down.

"We needed that *rain*," she said.

I thought about the people at the little church we went to when I was a girl, everyone always knowing what came next, which prayer, what page in the hymnal. The repetition and the knowing. There was a similar element of the repetitive and the known at the Cap, as if scenes and lines were delivered each morning to everyone, allowing time to rehearse. Everyone, except for me. It was starting to seem that I was there for the explicit purpose of being caught off guard.

"Raja is coming for lunch," Nikki said, as if it was an extension of her remark about the rain.

"Perfect," said Dasha.

Nikki said he would be landing at one. She said he had requested lobster.

And so Raja arrived precisely on time, though I was not waiting to greet him. I was in my room, packing. I had sent him a text after leaving the pool. I told him I had changed my mind, that I would be returning with him to Paris that day on the helicopter. He had not answered, but my mind was made up. Someone was not telling me the truth, I thought. And Dasha was suspicious. Suddenly, I didn't feel quite so safe and supported. I didn't feel like I was doing the *right* thing. What if everyone I had trusted so far had been lying to me all along. I told myself, *you can start over.* I told myself, *no one can hurt you.* I told myself, *you owe nothing to these people.* There was only one person I cared about that morning, and I did at least want to tell him goodbye. At what age are you old enough to know the people you think you love are people you don't really know at all.

I found him in the library, fiddling with tiny painted toy soldiers.

"Hi, you," he said, without even looking up. "How are you?"

"I think the real question is, how are *you*," I said.

"I am the same as always."

"Sweet, thoughtful, aware."

"*Dangerous*," he said. "That's what Dasha says. Dasha says a child is the most dangerous thing in the world."

The library seemed almost out of place in the compound. More formal than the other rooms, it easily held several thousand books. Whose books these were and whether anyone had ever opened them was unclear; the room went largely unused as far as I could tell, a desk in one corner empty except for a single framed photograph of the dogs. Entire shelves were filled with classical works of philosophy, history, and politics in English, but also

Russian and French. As Felix played silently, I walked over to a shelf with leather-bound volumes whose spines had neither titles nor authors, only the year stamped in gold on the spine.

"Do you prefer the present or the past," Felix said, breaking the trance of my curiosity. "I prefer the present. Dasha prefers the past. Nikki prefers the future."

"I don't know," I said. "I've never thought about it."

"I think people who have happy pasts prefer the past. Which makes sense. If you don't have a happy past, maybe you prefer the present. Or the future."

"I didn't have the happiest past," I said.

"I don't have a mother," he said, as he lay the soldiers in a precise line between us.

"I don't have a mother either."

The phrase shocked me as I said it, a confession unplanned. I had never talked about my mother. I had never talked about the crash. My entire experience with my mother could be summed up simply as, she was there, and then she was not. My uncles had planned a service, which was short and unremarkable. And it was only weeks later that I met Marcus. I would always remember that my mother died on a Tuesday, as Tuesdays I worked late. I had met Marcus on a Thursday, at a party to which I had been invited only the day before. Looking back, you can see a pattern in the facts, if you want. Looking back, I can see clearly how the lure of a new future was so acute, in those days. Planning a future in the wake of the death of your parents, when you're young, is less strategy than solution. There had been rumors about the crash being a suicide, a double suicide. How does any child move on after that.

Felix was standing right next to me. I could tell he was making an effort to control his emotions, that what I had said had moved him. As if I was the only one he had ever met who didn't have a mother either. For a child the death of a parent is the death of the hero before the story's even started.

"My mother died in a car crash," I said. "With my father. She was driving."

It was more than I had ever said out loud about it, even to Marcus.

To Marcus I had said something like, *we were never close.* Or did I say, *I prefer not to talk about it.*

It unnerved me that such recent memories were starting to slip, blur.

If you lived in the past did the past stay clear and accessible?

"I am sorry," Felix said.

"It's all right."

I told him not everyone has a mother who loves them deeply, who understands them, and who is, "to take your very fine word, 'present.'" I said I was sure Felix had inherited many of his mother's fine qualities, his intelligence for example, his fearlessness. In imagining his mother for Felix in that moment, I tried to imagine the mother I had wanted. In describing her to him I was listing the qualities of a woman I had never met, who never existed but who was, in that moment, essential for both of us. With that story of her I was mourning far more than our mothers.

Felix returned us both to earth by reaching for a large wooden chessboard and pulling it onto his lap.

"Will you play?"

"I don't play chess, I'm afraid."

My father told me when I was a girl that chess was a man's game.

"Women," my father said, "can't think that far ahead."

"I will teach you," Felix said with that absolute confidence.

And he had just about finished explaining the role of the bishop when the door opened.

"Lunch!" Nikki announced, like a train conductor.

Felix looked at her and didn't have to say a word, as the invisible hand of the Cap's teleology raised its index finger, reminding us all of the Cap's intractable chains of command. Nikki deferred to Dasha. Dasha deferred to Edouard. Edouard deferred to Felix and Felix, bless his heart, had not defined his allegiances yet. As Nikki turned to leave us, Felix slipped his small hand into mine.

I couldn't bear to tell him I had decided to leave.

I couldn't bear the idea that I might break his heart. Or break mine all over again.

*

Raja and Dasha and Nikki were waiting for us by a small round table under the pergola, the long one having been broken into sections and stored for the day. The small table was inlaid with white mosaic tiles in the shapes of stars indicating the major constellations. The table was a gift from a former Russian president for whom Edouard had babysat as a boy, a former Russian president Edouard had apparently taught to play ice hockey. The table sat six. That day, one seat would remain empty. Someone had indeed gone for lobsters that morning. They were already on the table, boiled and chilled, served over crushed ice with sides of bean salads, frites, and wine.

I had gone down to the kitchen just after dawn, ravenous. The morning sickness in the early months of pregnancy indicates, ironically, hunger. If you eat, the feeling subsides, and I had been making toast and eggs and oatmeal whenever I woke up, which was usually early. Sometimes, the kitchen was quiet. No one else seemed alive in the house until eight, when the children would come down for a meal before school.

In the kitchen everything was precisely organized. Even the "snack cupboard" filled with brightly colored sweets and black licorice, old-fashioned sugary gumdrops, and organic juice boxes. I had never seen Felix in the kitchen, but that cupboard must have been designed with him in mind.

When he saw him, Raja pulled Felix into a big bear hug.

"You're an old man," he said, and extended his palm on which sat, perfectly folded, a brand-new Arsenal T-shirt, which on closer inspection, had been signed by several players. Felix put the shirt on over the one he was wearing. It was enormous and dropped to his knees.

"A *nightshirt,*" said Raja.

He kissed me on one cheek and whispered in my ear, "Don't worry."

"Let's sit. We are so grateful for rain," Dasha said, before plates piled with even more arrived, before talk shifted to things like local politics, another impending rainstorm, Raja's thoughts on the state of the world.

For a moment, it felt normal.

Friends and family at a table for lunch.

I could see the surf breaks in the distance and the ever-present jet skis. Was their role less to keep anyone out than to prevent anyone from leaving. Any exit would upset the compound's equilibrium, like the absence of a bishop from the chess set.

While we ate, Felix and Raja talked sports while Nikki played with her phone and Dasha, as she so often did, sat in silence. When one of the teachers came to take Felix for class, Nikki excused herself. Someone brought three coffees and Raja and Dasha spoke about mutual friends, of how Dasha was now spending her days ("lots of reading" was the answer). Raja asked how Felix was doing and if there was any news on new treatments, at which point Dasha turned to me.

"We don't like to talk about it because we don't want to pathologize it, he's too little . . ." she said, then explained the issue, that his immune system was in the process of slowly breaking down, "a little like it does in HIV," and how he'd been born "with the same issue his mother had; it results in a certain fragility." She went on to say Felix's condition was "the main reason" they had come to the Cap, so they would be able to "control his environment." She went on to say that there was reason for optimism, that the speed of modern medicine's evolution meant there would likely be something he could take to slow the speed of the decline.

Raja took Dasha's hand.

"You're a strong woman," he said.

"There is no other kind," she said, and stood abruptly.

"I might have a swim before I go," he added, looking at me.

And the two of us were alone on the beach, looking up at the cliffs, when Raja let his hand slip into mine. I was open to various interpretations of the gesture. He hadn't said a word to me directly during lunch, or afterward on the walk upstairs, where a room had been prepared for him to change, as it once had been for me. I left him alone when his phone rang, and he arrived not long after at the path to the beach in one of Edouard's shirts, which was a little too large for him.

"You got my text," I said.

"I did."

"I'm leaving today."

"This is normal," he said, "what you're feeling, but we are so close to the end."

"The end of what."

"I can't tell you that, yet."

"We're close to the end, and you still can't tell me. I don't understand."

"You don't need to understand. You need—"

"Trust, faith, no. I need more information," I said.

"All right," he said. "Come on."

As we walked, he told me that "we" had intelligence Edouard was very sick.

"And I don't believe that. I see teachers here but not one nurse."

"I don't know what I'm doing here."

"What have you seen."

"A happy family."

"What about Edouard."

"What about Edouard."

I looked ahead to the rocky stairs I had climbed each of those nights, my walks with Edouard having grown subtly longer, slower, more deliberate. Our conversations ranging wider, growing increasingly intimate. A level of affection had developed. And wasn't that the goal, wasn't that, in fact, my job. And yet I wasn't sure how much of the truth of this would cause Raja to be pleased and how much of the truth of it might be reason for concern. That I might be, as Jack had put it, "a flight risk," that the early concern that I had not been properly vetted was coming home to roost. I was never a professional, I never pretended to be.

Raja walked ahead a few feet then turned and started walking backward, so slowly. I continued to walk forward, now facing him. He took my hands in his.

"Listen to me carefully," he said. "The truth is, we are in love."

"What."

"The truth is that Marcus and I were close friends, the *closest* of friends, but Marcus and I had a horrible falling out before he died, and on that night you and I had an affair. The *truth* is, I fell in love with you the minute I met you, in Paris, and it was mutual and it was dangerous and it was perfect."

We kept walking.

"But that is not true at all," I said.

"Well, I need you to believe it is true because it is the story going forward. It is your story, and it is the story they need in order to understand why you're really here, why you came."

"That we are in love."

"Yes."

"And that's why I am here."

"Yes."

Raja placed his hand on my stomach.

"That you're here because Marcus is dead and you're carrying my baby, but we cannot be together yet. You're here because I have asked you to be my wife and because we need time, a decent interval."

"A decent interval" sounded so clinical.

Raja stopped, leaned in, kissed my cheek.

He whispered in my ear.

"I have told Dasha. Do you understand."

What he wanted to know was not if I understood but if I could play along.

The last act is the most important.

The last act is the one they remember.

"I've already packed," I said.

"Well, you can unpack."

"No."

"Yes," he said, and he leaned in closer.

"Give me one reason to stay."

"Saving lives is a good way to spend your time."

He put his arm around my shoulders and pulled me toward him. If someone was watching us that day, they would have said they were watching a couple in love. A young woman, her unruly curls obscuring her face, the exotic white streak in her hair for which she'd been, according to Marcus, celebrated. If someone was watching, they might have described the woman as possessing a beauty that didn't knock you out but was there if you looked carefully. Anyone watching would have observed the older man with her, his dark skin, his physical charisma. Anyone watching would remember how he stood, in his bare feet, only a few inches taller. Might have noticed his shirt, which was too large, as if he'd borrowed it from an older brother. If someone was watching that couple they would certainly have remarked on an intimacy, a physicality, and from that they might have concluded that these two had in fact been together a long time, perhaps this moment was a reunion after a long absence. Anyone watching might even have described the couple as having behaved that day on the beach like teenagers. How the man walked ahead then turned around to face the woman, a kind of dance. Anyone watching might have speculated about a certain sadness between them. Did the woman appear upset. Was this not a reunion at all but rather a breakup, an ending, only the latest in a long line of losses they had each endured.

What was actually playing out on that beach that day was a lesson. It was on that beach that day that Raja had pulled me close and told me in careful, clear detail exactly who Edouard was, what Edouard had done, and what the costs would be if this operation failed. It was on that day that Raja had explained the operation would take place on the night of Edouard's birthday, that it was an "abduction," which meant no one would be hurt, and he'd said, "Trust me, we've done hundreds of these," that the goal was for Edouard to be "brought in" for questioning. If Edouard failed to answer questions, "The law will step in," Raja said. "The international justice establishment" has tools to elicit truth. The truth, Raja told me, would be a confession. A confession regarding American, British, and Israeli intelligence assets who had been, over a period of years while stationed in Beirut, assassinated.

The assassinations had been, Raja said, widely reported or papered with lies or, in at least one case, "disappeared," covered up, entirely denied. The assassinations targeted the exact assets Raja and his colleagues were in Beirut to recruit and run. Edouard's goal was to destroy the entire operation. Raja explained that the code shared by all the major intelligence services, that "We do not target our own," had been broken. And that, Raja said, was Edouard's fault. Raja assured me that Edouard was "still active," and that "We have high confidence Edouard is preparing to take down another network," this time one a little closer to home. Or more specifically, to *my* home. Edouard was planning the assassination of American assets based in the UK.

"All you have to do is ensure he attends the birthday." And he added, "This is what Marcus wanted." Marcus, who trained Raja and brought him back to Beirut. Marcus, who loved me. Marcus, the father of my child. And, as it had been at the Musée Rodin, my answer was clear before the question was asked.

"What about Felix," I asked.

"If you care about Felix, you do what we tell you."

The third act had begun.

The third act would open with a love story and close with a celebration.

*

If you were Dasha and had been watching the beach that day from the bedroom window, the one on the top floor, which was the one place she had privacy, you would have certainly noticed when and where he touched her, and how many times, whether she seemed to like it. The hand on her stomach, how he knelt down and carved a heart in the sand. If you were Dasha, you would also have been jealous. Dasha had not been touched, or even flirted with, in a very long time. Dasha at the window would have felt fury, too, because some clear bright bell of an instinct told her that while what she was seeing *looked* like love it was almost certainly something else entirely. Despite what Nikki had told her the day before, Dasha had a different view. She had perspective. And she had knowledge, accrued carefully and painfully over time, about Edouard and the kind of men who entered his world. Dasha, in her time, had starred in many third acts. Dasha had long ago ceased to believe in the existence of objective truth, the existence of order. Dasha knew anyone who came to the Cap was somehow related to "the magic show," as Edouard called it, the secret life. A life defined by an absence of one belief in the service of belief in something higher, the irony of that. Yes, if Dasha was watching from her window that day she would have been developing a new theory of exactly what was happening. Of what Raja wanted from her family. In Dasha's experience, everyone wanted something.

*

We reached the stairs. They were narrow enough that you had to climb single file. Raja went first, and held his head down, but kept talking. Unless someone had affixed a camera to his chest there was no way anyone could have heard what he said next.

"I've organized an account for the baby. Once you leave, I will be sure you're given access to it, and it will be all you both need to live a very, very happy life."

I could feel that my breath was shorter. Glancing to the left I saw the jet skis; now there were five, engines off, an arsenal at rest. What did they think about all day long out there. Which story had they been told. We were almost at the top when Raja stopped and reached back for my hand. He helped me up the last few steps and then, standing behind me, slid his hands around my waist, as if he were going to lift me up, a little girl placing a star atop the tree. We looked over the ocean just as I had done, many times, with Edouard. And then, in a way that would have been impossible for anyone behind us to see, he slipped a small piece of paper into my hand.

I slipped it into my pocket without opening it.

"What happened to Felix's mother," I asked.

"She died in childbirth."

Later, in the wake of conflicting emotions accompanying Raja's departure—fear, relief, exhaustion, gratitude, envy, guilt—I forgot about that piece of paper. Another sign of early pregnancy, the absolute atomization of short-term memory. The mind can be a careless cleaner and occasionally sweep out something essential. Why I had agreed to stay, I am not sure I will ever know. Raja made a convincing case. Raja said if I stayed, I would save lives. Raja said if I stayed, I would participate in history. Raja said Edouard was not at all what he appeared to be.

It was only lying in a very hot bath later that afternoon, staring at the hook on the back of the bathroom door, at the shirt of Edouard's Raja had worn, that I remembered the paper. I almost slipped rising quickly up out of the bath. Without drying off I shook the water from my hair and pulled my shorts off the floor. I opened it to read what Raja had written in his precise inimitable hand.

I LOVE YOU.

Documents like this supported the narrative, of course. The lies had to be indistinguishable from the "truths," which were in any event subjective, uncorralled, a risk. A story, on the other hand, can be airtight. A fine author crosses each *t* and dots every *i*. That "I love you" was a dotted *i*. Making love central to the story was inimitably Raja. He liked a romantic element. He felt it was a kind of insurance.

Jack was never romantic about the work. If Jack had a God that God was the lie, the story, the cover. Jack would say lying at close range isn't unnatural; people do it every day. Now, *killing* at close range, most people prefer not to. Jack would say you can train anyone to assemble a complex weapon, but you cannot teach them the courage to use it. Jack was "calm in trouble," to use Raja's phrase. The truth, though, speaking of, was that Jack's childhood had been defined by the folklore of lost IRA glory, by legends of heroes long dead by the time Jack was old enough to ride a bike. And by his grandfather's generation's celebrated choice of slaughter as a central tenet of their "organization's" foreign policy. His grandfather, who was rumored to have been a bombmaker. "War is diplomacy distilled," Jack told me once. It was little wonder how, when, or to what end Jack had landed in the "secret world." He had grown up inside it, after all.

I LOVE YOU.

That little piece of paper.

Those three words.

Did Raja love me? Even a little bit? Wasn't it necessary to feel some approximation of the truth to perpetuate the lie?

And did I love him.

I placed the tiny paper on my bedside table where anyone who happened to wander by could see it easily, a clue. The clue would be the first thing I saw when I woke up in the morning and the last thing I saw before closing my eyes at night. Raja, his eyes hidden behind dark glasses as we stood on the edge of the landing zone, my swimsuit still wet. Raja, clear on the *story*, had leaned in to say just as any young lover might, "Nothing will hurt you, or the baby." He said he would see me in a few weeks.

Birthday. DOB. DOB could be Date of Birth or Date of Burial. The beginning of a life or its end. I removed Edouard's shirt from the hook. I was thinking it would be kind of me to return it directly to him. It was almost time for our walk. I could say I thought it was time for me to come find him for a change.

*

Dasha's bedroom was the only one on the third floor. I had seen her room once, the day after my arrival, when Felix had taken me around the house, proud that he could show me something of interest, probably still unclear then about who I was or the chance of my introducing him to any celebrated football players. I would not have gone in, but her door was open. There were fresh roses on a bedside table.

"Dasha sleeps alone," Felix told me.

"Some people like to sleep alone," I said, as if I had to make it make sense for him.

"Some people like their space, you mean," he said, which made me laugh. Felix, like Raja, always knew just what to say.

"Where does your father sleep," I asked, then immediately regretted it. But the thing is, Felix only saw innocence in me, I truly believe that. For Felix, I was the good stranger, the one who came to heal. I was not one of the long line of foreigners who arrived at all hours with requests or favors. I was not one of the "cousins," if they even were cousins. The other children who came in and out of the compound seemed neither as smart nor as sensitive as Felix. They likely annoyed him with their less-than-stellar passing and kicking skills, their absence of deep knowledge of the game. The "truth" of Felix was that Felix was nine going on twenty-nine and would, it occurred to me more than once in those days, have made a far more formidable asset for Raja to run. Maybe Raja knew that, maybe that knowledge was part of Raja's project to charm Felix, keep him close. "A relationship is the only currency you cannot hedge," Raja said.

"My father usually sleeps outside the house," Felix said.

"*Outside?*" I imagined Edouard lying in the grass, staring up at the stars.

"Yes, he has the coolest room. Would you like to see it?"

He led me down the stairs and through the foyer, past the enormous carved wooden Chinese chairs just as candles were being lit in preparation for sunset. We walked across the porch and then around to the back of the house. As we entered the grove of lemon trees, I remembered taking the exact same walk with Nikki, on my first visit to the Cap. And suddenly I knew where we were going. We were going toward the paintings.

"I have seen your father's paintings," I said.

"A very famous man painted those. And then he died."

"Yes."

"My father says they remind him of home."

"Isn't *this* home?"

"Oh, this will never be home, this is just a transition. That's what my father says. When I turn ten, we're moving to Paris. I turn ten in January. I was born in a snowstorm."

"Paris is lovely," I said, as if I knew. As if I wasn't thinking about all that might happen before Felix turned ten.

And I could see the museum up ahead, its imposing black door glimmering with the appearance of having been newly painted, or perhaps cleaned. Felix walked up to the door and entered the code. I could hear five short beeps, so there were five numbers in the code. I remembered that from the time before because five is an unusual number for a code, codes are usually evenly numbered, four or six or eight or ten. The door opened and we entered, and it was all exactly as before. Felix waited a minute while I walked across the space, those little lights coming on one by one in my wake, until I was at the far end of the room. I turned and looked at him.

"He sleeps here?"

"No. He sleeps *here*," said Felix, and he walked over to a door I hadn't noticed before as it was painted the same color as the walls, there was no doorknob, it was almost invisible. Felix pressed on the door, but it was locked. And so he knocked, which made me nervous, though I was curious to see what was on the other side. He knocked again, and called for his father, but no one came.

"We will try again later," he said. "I think you will really like it."

*

So I knew where Edouard would be. I knew, too, that Edouard trusted me. And so it made absolute sense to return the shirt Raja had worn. And yet as I stood at the entrance to the "museum," I remembered the one thing I did not know—the code.

I thought about Jill's long legs and how many men, and women, she'd distracted with them. "Jill's our killer angel," Raja said, as the small ceiling fan spun anticlockwise in the hotel. *Parisiennes* don't like air-conditioning.

"She doesn't like me," I said.

"Jill doesn't like *anybody*. So you're in excellent company."

"She likes you," pressing, testing.

"Oh, she definitely does not like *me*," Raja said, and though his eyes were closed he was smiling. "Jill prefers women over men, number one. Jill never sleeps with spies, which by the way is a wise rule, number two. Though even if she did," and he turned on his side and looked at me, "number three, she's too tall for my taste.

"You worry too much, kid," he said, and it was the first time he called me that but would not be the last.

"People don't like to think of women in war," he said, suddenly serious. "To imagine a woman's capacity for violence."

*

And as I stood there, about to turn back, the door opened. Edouard was wearing reading glasses, which I had never seen him do. They made him look older, a nod to vulnerability. On seeing me, he smiled.

"I was just about to come to find you," he said.

I held out his shirt.

"Raja borrowed this," I said, as if deflecting blame.

Stay with facts.

Stay away from feelings.

"Come in. I want to show you my favorite."

He walked to a canvas directly opposite the door to his room.

On seeing them now for a third time I was struck by the repetition of circles in the paintings. Circles of all sizes, in varying colors, used in different ways on each canvas. Looking closely at any one of them, I could discern certain recognizable figures, a mythic beast with a lion's body and a man's helmeted head, for example. I could start to see the shapes of what appeared to be weapons—a sword, a shield, a mace. Edouard stood in front of a canvas I hadn't noticed before. I went to stand with him and could see clearly that it was different from the others. I could make out a woman's figure. She was staring up at the sky and I could see, inside three large circles that might have been clouds, a set of almost imperceptible dots.

"They're stars," Edouard said.

The woman wore a crown of ribbons in her hair.

"What do you think of her," Edouard said.

"I don't know what to think," I replied, which was true.

"What do you notice that's different about her."

"I don't know."

"Where is she looking?"

"Up."

"The painting is called *Portrait of a Warrior*."

"She doesn't look like a warrior."

"No, she does not. She is looking up to God to beg mercy for her son."

And I understood.

"It's Hector's mother."

Edouard turned and looked at me, a teacher proud of his student. He had told me he'd asked the painter to "divine a sense of the *Iliad*'s atmosphere," and I had asked what he meant, and he'd said, "a beautiful, terrifying chaos, what all wars feel like." He took the shirt from my hand and threw it casually onto the same small chair Nikki had sat in.

*

After our walk, during which we'd barely talked, Edouard left me at the front of the house and said he was going for a swim. "You can come see the paintings anytime," he said. I watched him walk away and wondered if he was lonely. Edouard didn't have friends imported to play football with him. I was halfway back to my room when I turned around, walked back down the stairs and around to the back of the house, through the lemon grove and to the museum.

You can come see the paintings anytime.

I stood at the door and looked at that tiny keypad. Five numbers. Or was it five letters *linked* to numbers? Dasha has five letters. Nikki has five letters. And so does Felix. I tried Felix first, and as I tapped the *x,* linked to number nine, I heard the click. Easy, transparent, obvious. Perhaps that was the point. A code a young boy can remember, *like his own name.* One day that code would be part of the story of Felix's childhood, a sign of love from his father, a small detail to hold on to long after Felix had left the Cap, moved far away to "normal life," social life, relationships. After he had learned several languages and read Russian history deeply, and all the Russian novels. After, as a young man, Felix would gain an even deeper respect and admiration for who his father had once been. After Felix took time to visit Moscow, to meet "the old guard," and hear their stories about the man he had known mainly from bedtime stories and the football pitch, the man who liked licorice but only on occasion. After Felix understood that his father's life had been anything but leisurely, that the question of what would be served for dinner at the Cap had never been the most important question of Edouard's day.

F-E-L-I-X

And I was inside.

Entering the space, I could see Edouard's shirt on the chair, exactly where he left it.

I walked to the bedroom door.

I knocked.

And then I opened it, and simply stepped inside.

*

Marcus loved a book that had belonged to his finca's prior owner. It sat on a table in the living room in Spain. It was called *JEF-FERSON AT MONTICELLO* and inside, in addition to images of the early American President's immaculate, terraced Virginia gardens and the original plans for his house's architecture and design, there was a series of images of Jefferson's bedroom. Jefferson's bed, tucked into an alcove perfectly enclosing it, creating a kind of architectural canopy, was so strange, something I had never seen before.

"Now, that's the kind of bed you sleep in to atone for your sins," Marcus said, adding that Jefferson had many, *"many, many"* sins. Marcus added, more seriously, that only someone committed to sleeping alone would design a bed like that.

"Maybe he simply liked the way it looked," I had said.

"And maybe he felt it was a way to never have to commit," he'd said. "No woman would sleep in a bed like that."

Marcus always made me see things differently.

Marcus liked his space, too. The last thing Marcus would want is a ceiling over his bed close enough that he could touch it. Marcus thought Monticello, while inarguably something to behold on the outside—"there is no greater green," he had said, giving nature the lead credit—was "a little like a prison, a very elegant prison" on the inside. Only Marcus could consider Monticello a prison. That early American aesthetic was too punishing, in his view, even though he leaned toward a level of restraint in his own taste. Marcus told me, when he saw me reading the book, that he had been to Monticello. "Baby, I'm from Virginia, Monticello is our Mecca." He told me that during his time working in Washington he would often drive to Charlottesville on weekends just to walk in the foothills of the Blue Ridge Mountains, to "get out of the asylum," as if I could understand what that meant. Marcus knew everything about the history of Virginia and told me once that, as a boy, all he'd wanted was to live there forever, "be an East Coast cowboy, a mountain man." I knew very little about America before I met Marcus. America, to a younger me, was open, expansive, wild, free. The last word I would have thought of when thinking of America, or her Founding Fathers, was "prison."

And yet America is, in the end, an open book. America can be tracked in facts and maps. America can be known. If I had taken time then to think about what I knew to be true of Marcus, I would have had to admit I knew only what he had told me plus what I had assumed based on a small, select set of actions. Based on what I chose to observe when he was alive. The Marcus I had made up my mind to love was light and broad and fast, voracious for life and casually spoiled, magnanimous. It never occurred to me that there was an entirely different Marcus, one I could never know, one not tracked by facts or maps, one entirely traceless and un-Google-able. It never occurred to me that Marcus had spent decades trying on different roles and that the role of my husband, while neither complex nor exotic, was his final and most important performance. Marcus and I never talked about our childhoods, but even if I had asked, I doubt he would have shared. I doubt he would have told me, for example, that he was raised by a single mother who worked as a cleaning lady for a local landowner, how she spent her weekends as a docent at Monticello. And how this was the real reason Marcus knew Jefferson's home intimately, the real reason he considered it a prison. Marcus would not have shared how his father died in Vietnam only days before the Saigon evacuation, not as a hero but in an accident, having wandered into a bar fight at the wrong time, leaving a young widow and her young son back in Charlottesville. I would never know that Marcus's father's life had been defined by war, that he had been a foreign service officer, a job Marcus would consider a cog in a broken machine. How could I have guessed that before Marcus was old enough to drive, he had formed an ironclad narrative of his family defined by loss and accidents, a narrative he would set out to avenge by choosing work he thought meaningful, defined by missions and rules, redlines and citations and maps. Marcus enlisted in the army in his last year of high school, then rose through the special operations ranks before transitioning to the CIA's elite paramilitary division, a division whose work you will never hear about, speaking of traceless, led by men less interested in power than in things like hostage rescues and "foreign internal defense." A division, ironically, defined by accidents and losses. And by a government that would never officially acknowledge its successes, yet rigorously deny its failures. If I had known even one of those things, I might have understood Marcus

differently. And if I had known it all I would have loved him even more. I would have seen myself in his story.

*

Edouard's room was small, with no windows. On a desk crowded with papers was a photograph of two young men, their arms around each other's shoulders, smiling. I looked closer and felt a physical jolt. There he was, looking back at me, "my late husband" as I was only then learning to say. There he was, years before we met, his hair entirely absent those streaks of gray. The other man in the photograph, next to Marcus, was a man I didn't recognize, wearing what looked like an American military uniform, a tiny flag patch on its shoulder. On his shirt pocket was a label with a name: BARNES. They looked happy. I looked closer and noticed a street sign behind them, in French. Was the photograph taken in Paris. Marcus had never mentioned anyone called Barnes, and Marcus had been so specific about all the times he had visited France before we were there, together. He had told me about his very first visit, as a boy, to Biarritz. And later the exchange program in high school near Nice. He told me he had seen Paris many times for work "in my twenties and thirties," but I had never asked for more detail. Asking felt like prying. I'd imagined him without me and before me. I'd pictured him in conference rooms and restaurants. I'd imagined him with other women. I had not imagined him outside the lines of the man he himself had drawn for me, or ever doubted that drawing's accuracy. Why would I.

At the center of the room was a near-exact replica of Thomas Jefferson's Monticello bed. I walked to the bed, mindful of time passing, and looked inside the alcove. On the wall at the foot of

Edouard's bed was another framed photograph. A young woman on a beach. She looked straight into the camera. She was smiling with a slyness I immediately recognized, and so immediately understood: she was Felix's mother. As I looked closer, I could see her bright green eyes, a similar green to my own. And I could see, at the center of her unruly curls, also similar to mine, she had something else: a bright, white streak. A birthmark.

You were born for this, Marcus had said.

She saved my life, more than once, Edouard had said.

Plausible deniability, Jack had said.

The photograph was the first thing Edouard saw when he woke up in the morning, and the last thing he saw before he closed his eyes at night.

*

As I came through the lemon grove I ran into Edouard.

He was dripping wet, a towel around his waist, barefoot, the whole nine yards of cool.

He stopped, as if he could tell I was in shock.

"Were you looking for me?" he said.

His phone rang and he answered it, holding up his hand for me to wait.

I felt like I had committed a crime, which in a way I had.

I felt that I knew more about him than he did about me. Without hanging up, Edouard hit mute and I could hear a male voice speaking in what sounded like Russian on the other end. Edouard looked at me, focused. And amused, like a child proud to be doing two things at once.

"My son is very taken with you," he said, talking about himself, and now I knew exactly why.

"I am very taken with him."

I wondered if Felix, like his father, had seen that photograph enough times to have committed it to memory. If Felix felt an alarming lack of coincidence in the striking similarity between his mother, whose name was Sophie, and me. Had Dasha seen it and had Nikki. Had I been wandering around their lives less like a widow and more like a ghost. And I wondered if Marcus, all the way back at that party in London the night we had met, had seen Sophie in me, and what that meant. And suddenly the things I thought I knew to be true, about why I was there, and what I was doing, started to slip the mooring of available evidence. If life was a math problem mine would no longer compute. I tried imagining all possible explanations. Coincidence, for example, an excellent guard against horror. In fact, if you had asked me that day what I thought Sophie, beautiful Sophie, Felix's mother and Edouard's great love, and I had in common I might have said, simply, that we had both been in love. We had both once been in love with a complicated man.

When the truth slaps you in the face it takes time to regain your composure.

"Very taken," Edouard added, before turning away from me and toward his prison.

What if my resemblance to a woman I had never met was an accident.

What percentage of women are born with white streaks in their hair.

What if a comfort *is* a prison.

What if a lie is the key to the truth.

I stopped by the kitchen on the way to my room to tell the cook I was not feeling well. I asked to have dinner upstairs. I went to my bathroom, turned on the shower, and opened my phone.

I Googled "Taran Davies Barnes American military" to find a single entry, a brief notice from *Al Balad,* a Lebanese newspaper:

[American Embassy Official Dead in Car Crash]

Tracy Barnes, 38, an American diplomat, died early Tuesday morning when his car hit a telephone pole near the American University. A decorated veteran, Barnes will be buried at Arlington National Cemetery, in Washington, D.C. In a statement released by the embassy, a colleague, Taran Davies, said simply, "Tracy was the best of us."

The article was dated nine years ago.

This was the only reference to Tracy Barnes I found anywhere, ever.

If Barnes existed at all he failed to exist online.

I sat there for a long time, the bathroom filling with the shower's heat, reading and rereading that notice, looking for any clue, any path, any error, imagining which facts were held back. By trying to imagine who Tracy Barnes was, and his death and that day, I was trying to imagine Marcus, too. What else had he endured. And how it was, or was not, a coincidence my host not only had a photograph of my late husband on his desk but also had not, in all our time together, ever related his ideas about "loss" to the one man we both knew.

Edouard had never once asked about my husband, never even asked his name. And though we had talked about history and literature and his childhood and mine, about Felix, and the Cap cook's best and worst dishes, and why Edouard preferred the west coast of France ("It's wilder, west coasts always are"), about the killing of the Romanovs and the meaning of perestroika, Edouard had never once asked anything about my marriage. If I had thought about the strangeness of that before seeing the photograph of Marcus on his desk, I would have said the elisions were manners. I would have defended Edouard as "discreet." I would have assured you there was something elegant about the absence of cruder curiosity in his character. I remember putting my phone down and stepping into the shower. I remember because that shower was the first time in a long time that I had cried.

When I opened the bathroom door, Felix was sitting on my bed.

"Oh, hello," I said.

"Hello, you."

Was there a neon sign on my forehead flashing my emotions, my sadness, alarm.

Was he seeing his mother when he looked at me.

"I heard you're not feeling well," he said. "And that's no fun."

I went to the bed and sat down next to him.

"No, it really is not."

"I don't feel well a lot of the time," he said. "I find it's better when I'm lying in bed."

"Oh, everything is better when lying in bed," I said, which was something Marcus had once said when I had asked how he could work from bed, how anyone could possibly think clearly while lying down. Marcus called the bedroom in Mallorca "the war room." He would say, "I have a meeting in the war room" or, "It's essential we discuss this in the war room." I wouldn't realize until later that this habit had soldered an unconscious connection in my mind between the words "war" and "bed."

"Can I keep you company," said Felix. "I won't bother you."

He started playing chess on his phone. I closed my eyes and fell into a deep sleep, and into another dream. I was with Marcus, only it was Marcus from the photograph, younger Marcus, leaner, closer to my age. It was Marcus, but he was dressed like Edouard, the linen shirt and swimming trunks. We were holding hands and dangling our feet over the side of a wide, wooden dock. The tide was high, and the ocean was rough, and I could feel waves lapping my toes through my sandals. The water was cold. And the cold, plus tiny white lights strung along the dock's posts, indicated it was Christmastime. Someone was playing carols, and I could hear "The Little Drummer Boy." And though Marcus was singing along—*a newborn king to see pa rum pum pum pum*—I couldn't hear him. As if I were less in the dream than watching myself in it. As if the dream were a television set to mute. I could not hear anything, though I knew what was being said. And then looking down, past my feet, I could clearly see a shadow of something moving in the water. Some dangerous beast, I was sure, or not just any shark but a *Jaws*-sized shark, a dinosaur, a submarine. I tried to warn Marcus, but he simply kept singing, and laughing, and then he hung his arm over my shoulder, exactly as his arm had been hung over the shoulder of Tracy Barnes in the photograph on Edouard's desk. And his arm suddenly felt heavy, and then heavier and heavier until it was like a steel beam boring into my back, like it would crush me. As Marcus leaned over to kiss my ear, I could see the beast start to rise out of the water and—

"Are you all right," said Felix.

I had cried out. I had scared myself awake. I had scared Felix, too.

"I was having a dream."

"About what?"

"About my husband," I said.

My late husband.

"What was his name."

"Taran. His name is Taran. His name was Taran."

IX

ILIUM

Early on the morning of Edouard's birthday, I later learned, Jack and Jill were in a small green Citroën driving from Paris to Arcachon, while Annabel was boarding a helicopter in Toulouse, which would land not at the compound, but on a nearby property the team had secured for the night. That property would serve as the "staging location" the team would use to prepare for "Evening," as they were calling it. "Evening" is a gentler, more humane word than, for example, the very clinical "operation." Evening implied rest, darkness, silence. Evening implied an end.

Jill liked precision. Jill, like Jack, had a sense of humor, which in a way one has to have in their line of work. Whenever Jack and Jill had a job that involved "kinetic activity," they referred to the work simply according to the time of day in which it would take place. "April Morning" was what they called the project they had been engaged for outside Istanbul. "Winter Tea" was how they talked about those three days in Dakar. "Evening" would be their code for the Arcachon operation, and Evening did not need a modifier. It was that important, singular. Evening was perhaps the *most* important job Jack and Jill had ever, and would ever, take part in. What happened at Arcachon would have consequences for men and women Jack and Jill would never meet. Historic, yet invisible consequences. Evening, one of only a handful of seminal intelligence operations, would ensure lives were saved. Like the car crash in Beirut, Evening wouldn't be written up in any newspaper. Evening, if successful, would be traceless, un-Google-able, a masterpiece made with invisible ink. The story of Arcachon, and Evening, would be parsed in private rooms populated by diplomats, special operators, and other "interested parties." Evening, those who had heard about it would say over Château d'Yquem or Wild Turkey, depending on the location, was a black swan, a fairy tale, a work of art.

Raja's office had given Arcachon a more formal name, one in keeping with the unit's traditions. Raja knew that what was going to take place at the compound that night was, in fact, a classic variation on a theme, and he believed all classic operations need names aligned with either a play at national pride or a nod to the target. Raja knew that on that night he would be participating in history. And so for Raja, Edouard's birthday would always be not only the DOB of an elusive former Russian general, killer, and proud, loving father, but also the DOB of Operation Ilium. It would be Ilium back at Langley on the seventh floor, and Ilium when it landed on C's desk at MI6. Ilium was not a nod to the Trojan War, though, as many believed. Ilium was not named after Edouard's paintings. Ilium was a scriptural reference to the biblical idea that there is a "time to kill." That there is such a thing as a moral vengeance. Raja believed any brutal, violent action that would take place at Arcachon was an act of God's grace. Ilium, in the end, was a philosophical stance.

*

Jack and Jill had a busy day ahead of them. Ilium was a covert, "deniable" operation, which meant that if anything went wrong, blame would be taken solely by the team. A team with no clear ties to any nation state or government, a team whose members' names and addresses had changed so many times over the last decade that, remarkable in an era when information was porous and unprotectable, they had almost entirely traceless lives. Jack and Jill had been hired by Raja for exactly this reason, and it was not the first time he had used them, so there was a level of trust, comfort, shorthand. Even Raja did not know their true identities, and he did not care.

Jack and Jill and Annabel didn't mind violence, but what they really loved was money, and there are very few lines of work in which you're as richly compensated. And though they'd spent weeks on the job, which was a long time, Raja had spent almost a decade. It was only a year earlier that Raja had believed he had exhausted all his options. A year earlier the CIA's official support was starting to recede. Bureaucracies think like accountants, and the line item that was "Edouard" had long since ceased to make sense inside the Agency. Even inside Russia House there were many who, in the years before Arcachon, believed Edouard was dead or else winding down his days with prostitutes in Lamu, or Saint John; at least they'd been right about his preference for beaches. Raja believed otherwise. Raja had religion about finding Edouard because, for Raja, it was personal. The idea that the mission to find, and interrogate, Edouard would lack completion was tearing Raja up inside a year before Ilium; he could not let it go. And yet with each day, new "clearer and more present" threats arose around the world, sexier dragons to slay. A different generation took over international intelligence with a new set of ideas. For them, the wars Raja had fought in were runic follies. For them the idea that an aging Russian posed a threat to America, or to anyone, seemed absurd.

"You have to bring this one over the one-yard line," was the last thing Marcus said to Raja before he died. "Bring it over the one-yard line, and take care of her." And though by the time he died Marcus had long since ceased being Raja's handler, Raja experienced that as an order. Raja had flown one final time to America and driven to Langley, to plead in person to the Director of the CIA. Raja had the outlines of the plan. It wasn't perfect, but it was close. He had a location, a goal, a budget. He had the start of a team. And he wasn't asking for much, no close air support, no fancy toys, no quick response team, no paramilitaries. The Director, as luck would have it, had come up through Russia House, had served in Moscow and Kyiv and other Eastern European stations. He understood the implications and had been raised on the legend of OSS operators during World War II. And he had always liked Raja. It's not often a foreign national, recruited by the CIA as an asset, evolves into one of its finest officers. When Raja closed his presentation with, "There will not be one American life lost," the Director said, "Do not fuck this up."

Then over dinner with Annabel at Billy Martin's in Georgetown, Raja had shared the outlines of the idea and its problems, and Annabel had replied as if he had asked for an aspirin. "Oh, I have a solution to that." The solution was a phone number, which she had entered into Raja's mobile under the name "Bono," and that was Jack. She'd added, "You'll also need an orphan," which at first Raja didn't understand, but once she explained it he could see it clearly, why her way was the way to go. "Do you know a good orphanage?" he'd asked, and Annabel had nodded, of course she did. "I know an orphanage, and I know an expediter." She promised to give him a deal.

*

Raja pretended to dislike war. Raja would say, if you'd asked him in the months leading up to Ilium, that he was "a warrior in repose," that any wars he'd once fought in were now long behind him and forgotten. But the wars had never receded for him at all, in particular what had happened to his friend Tracy. In fact, since the death of Tracy Barnes in Beirut one wintry morning near the entrance to the American University, Raja and Marcus had been clear on this: they would, one day, find a way to "make it right." In fact, while they never talked about it in quite this way, Raja and Marcus both felt they owed the lives they had lived since that day in no small part to Tracy. Tracy, who would never again eat a lobster in Paris, or anywhere else. Tracy, who would never let his new bride beat him on an ocean swim in the Balearics, never amass a fortune in business, never carve a heart in the sand. Tracy, the bravest among them, who'd died for their sins. Tracy, who loved fast cars and dreamed of one day retiring to a "quiet life" as a Formula One driver, who would say his finest skill was his ability to navigate a sharp turn at ninety miles an hour. You might have said Tracy's death in a car crash was ironic. Only there was nothing ironic about the crash that killed Tracy, because the crash was not a crash at all. It was an assassination.

What the reporter from *Al Balad* had failed to ask the local police was not one thing, but anything at all. The reporter, a young Lebanese woman who had graduated with a First in Greats from Oxford and had her own political ambitions, had received a text from her boss while swimming laps at the Beirut Four Seasons, having been asked to review the pool. She wasn't usually called in on car crashes. She wasn't usually called in on anything important because her boss had hit on her once and she'd rejected him. If in fact her boss had ever seen his young reporter as capable of fine work, he hid it artfully, cloaking resentment in sexism, a stance less shameful, less *childish*. And so, when his text said to come to his office immediately about "an urgent matter," and when he had handed her the paragraph he had written, she simply nodded. What else could she do. He told her not to change a word, and to run it under her byline. Even though the reporter considered herself a gifted writer and even though she wanted to look into the story, she never did. Even after sources at La Sûreté Générale confirmed the "officer" in the accident was American CIA. Her boss, the editor, dismissed the rumors. He boasted of doing so later at his Tuesday night poker game, where the other players included the Beirut chief of police, Mossad's senior-most man on the ground, and two Russian "pharmaceutical executives." The Russians provided sworn, if forged, affidavits claiming Barnes had an addiction problem. The Russians wrote, in their sworn statement, that they themselves had *provided* the drug, evidence of which was found in Barnes's apartment. Which was odd as Tracy Barnes had been sober since college. An autopsy was never performed.

*

Jack and Jill were veterans of so many wars they'd lost count. Trying to count would depend on a clear definition of what war was, and there hadn't been that clarity in a generation. Jack and Jill had never been lovers but had grown to be like siblings, completing each other's sentences, forgiving bad habits. Clear in the knowledge they would each kill to save a life for the other if required. Hence their choice of cover names that indicated partnership, not romance. They had both worked, essentially, as mercenaries from a very young age. It is a job it will not surprise you to know does not get much respect, and yet gets ample misunderstanding. Jack and Jill weren't in it for respect, though, not by the time the green Citroën sped toward the French coast, Jill lazily exhaling her Gauloises out the window. Had Jack been born at another time in another place, he might have founded a Silicon Valley unicorn or become a Pulitzer Prize–winning investigative journalist. The hunt was all for Jack. And Jill of course could have gone into any line of work that banked on her exotic looks, as an actress or a model or a certain kind of rich man's wife, though her real gift would have been wasted. Jill's gift was with interrogation and negotiation, skills required uniquely during what Raja called "the messy close." Jill wasn't quite what most people think of when they think of a clean-up crew, but when *persuasion* was involved, when making the case for risky choices under pressure was involved, you called Jill. If you could afford her. When a lightning storm threatens the landing zone. When a politician shoots his mistress, and misses. Jill didn't need to wave fancy weapons around. She was the fancy weapon. And this was what Annabel had explained to Raja, not at Billy Martin's but later, back in Beirut. On *that* visit she'd brought him another gift. A photograph of a young boy with enormous eyes, wearing a Turkish football jersey.

"Who's this," Raja asked.

"This," she'd said, "is your insurance."

Annabel provided Jack and Jill what she provided all her clients, a cross-section of the international underworld, what might be called "marketing." Annabel's gift was that she knew people who knew people. Annabel was at ease in the "real" world of office visits to McKinsey or Goldman Sachs, places where people still wore suits and had casual pretensions of "legitimate" power. Annabel knew who manned the night desk at the DGSE, but she also knew the maître d' at the bar with no name in Sanaa. Annabel lived in between. Everyone at a certain level of any international intelligence agency seemed to have had *some* experience of Annabel, whether over dinner on a kibbutz on the Syrian border or over Christmas tea at Claridge's. Businessmen whose careers were in one way or another "intelligence adjacent" knew her, too. Most men might think the idea of a female international fixer is a lie, a chimera, a myth cooked up by aspiring spy novelists. Annabel wasn't like most women. She eschewed deep attachments, and, as Marcus once put it, "eats boyfriends for breakfast."

Two nights before the morning of Edouard's birthday, Raja had taken the team out to thank them, and to thank Annabel in particular, "Annabel, who traveled the farthest to be here with us, because she came from heaven." Raja knew the value of knowing Annabel and of having her services on demand. Raja had helped Annabel build her networks, and it was Raja who was the one to pitch Annabel's plan to Marcus, who, when presented with its clear logic, would reluctantly agree. That reluctance was what lay beneath Marcus asking me, on the morning of our wedding, if I wanted to call it all off. He wasn't quite trying to warn me, he was indicating that things might not be what they seem. He was opening the door. He was breaking protocol. Asking if I wanted to call it all off was throwing me a lifeline, even though he prayed that I wouldn't take it. And of course I didn't. The next time you throw me a lifeline, please call it what it is.

What Raja, and later Marcus, understood immediately was that I was the perfect one for the job. Not only did I look the part I was, coincidentally, what every case officer dreams to find in an asset: naïve, no strong ties, poor. I didn't even know myself, the ultimate vulnerability. I was, Raja assured Marcus, even before he'd ever laid eyes on me, "entirely open to new experiences, like a child" and "apparently absent basic curiosity," by which Raja meant, not prone to pry. Yet the coup de grâce was my looks. After a photograph of Sophie was shared, one of Annabel's Piccadilly Circus spies had spotted and assessed me on the Tube before calling in Raja to confirm the choice one rainy day in Central London. Then later calling in Marcus to attend the party where we met. The only error in their plan was the only error there ever is in espionage. Love. Marcus and Raja had been waiting a long time to find me. When love arrived, they weren't about to let it get in the way. Raja had been counting the days. Only children count days, you might say. Children in advance of a holiday, the dream of freedom. Children, and prisoners.

"I love her," Marcus told Raja the morning of our wedding. "Sorry about that."

"God help her."

"God help *us,* my friend. God help us."

In the years after Marcus "retired" from government service, he had built a real business career, still "helping out" his friends at the Agency on the margins but under the nonofficial cover of a successful investment business born of his unique capability to travel to places most businessmen don't like to go. For all his pretend love of comfort, Marcus was happiest surviving on bread and water in a tent, as some deals would require. "The deal," an investor's variation on "the mission." And Marcus had seen his share of tents before he met me. He had always wanted a simpler, if lonelier, life, defined by friendship, by Raja and their old friend Tracy. If Marcus had ever wanted to cut ties entirely from the secret life, Tracy's death had prevented that. The loss kept him engaged, as is often the case.

*

On the morning of his birthday, Edouard opened his bedroom door to find Felix standing there, holding a cupcake, and a matchbook, waiting for someone to offer a third hand to help light the tiny tricolor candle planted firmly in icing the cook had made from scratch. Old-fashioned icing, thick and buttery, laced with vanilla extract. I know this because, later, after everything was over, precise reports were filed of who was where, and when, throughout that day. Dasha had reported, with no emotion, that she had argued with Felix in the kitchen not long after dawn, telling him the last thing his father would want would be any disturbance of his morning routine. Edouard didn't like live human contact, she told Felix, before his important midday meetings. Edouard liked his mornings to prepare, or swim, to think. And on that morning, Edouard would especially need his silence and "space" before that evening's party, which in truth Dasha knew well Edouard was mixed about. Edouard abided it to placate Dasha. Dasha had begun to tire of their time in the compound; she had begun to, as Edouard put it, "scratch at the door." Edouard also abided it, I think, for me. I liked parties well enough, he now knew. Edouard, if I had to guess, was looking forward to seeing my happiness that night. When he woke up that morning and looked at her photograph, who did he see.

"Oh, everyone wants a cupcake on their birthday," Felix protested.

The cook laid the icing especially thick on one cupcake and handed it to Felix.

"There will be plenty of cake tonight," was Dasha's argument, entirely missing the point.

Though she had raised a daughter, Dasha didn't understand children. Children rarely respond to rational argument.

"He knows *that*, but *this* will be a surprise. Everyone likes surprises."

"Ha, not your father," said Dasha, which was true.

But Felix was confident in one thing, which was that the decision was his to make, so he gave Dasha the impression for about six seconds that he was thinking it over before walking out of the kitchen and, as she could see clearly, in the direction of the back garden.

"That child," she'd said to the cook, "is spoiled."

"I think he may simply be lonely," said the cook and offered a cupcake to Dasha, who, having probably never eaten a cupcake, politely declined.

Dasha had a busy day ahead, too. Though the party would be under the pergola at the long table, and the majority of the guests were people they knew well and whom she could seat with her eyes closed, one very important guest was arriving today, all the way from Moscow, and the logistics of getting him there and on time had not been uncomplicated, or cheap. This guest, Dasha felt, was the solution to a problem. This guest was going to offer Edouard a very special "position" back in Moscow, one it would be almost impossible for him to refuse. This would mean an end to the idyll at the Cap. And it would mean a new beginning for Dasha. It might even mean she could start over.

Dasha had rooms prepared for sessions of rest for the guests before dinner. She had decided, she would later say, on a simple supper of spaghetti Bolognese followed by salted fish, and chocolate cake at the end, Edouard's favorite. Then everyone would go down to the beach, for a twenty-two-minute firework show set to *Swan Lake*. Dasha knew that casual extravagance was what her guests expected, the *quiet* extravagance of a spectacle designed to dazzle ten thousand but which would be, in this case, performed for thirty not counting staff or children. Each detail of the party had been decided on by a Dasha deeply tired of living in exile, tired of only ever dressing in a swimsuit, silently mourning a life she had left and would never recover, perhaps mourning an aging husband, a petulant daughter, a stepson she would never control. If there was one person who was truly lonely at the Cap it wasn't Felix, it was Dasha. Dasha was the one used to disappointment. And part of Dasha was aware that, since my arrival, her marriage was cooling at a faster pace.

Many marriages are marriages of convenience, or transaction, and though no one says they like a gold digger, the truth about people who marry for reasons other than love isn't binary. The truth is that anyone can endure whatever marriage they have chosen and will construct elaborate lies to survive it. And denial works wonders. It is only when you call a thing what it is that pain swims swiftly to the surface. It was only when Dasha looked at Edouard, only hours before the party, and said, "You've never loved me," that, for a second, she was vulnerable and felt something for him. And he felt something for her, too. They made love that afternoon, the first time in almost a year. Afterward he said, and he meant it, "I've always loved you, you idiot." He waited a while before adding, "Just not in the way you deserve to be loved."

As Dasha and the cook made a final review of the menu, Nikki lay in bed listening to a book about Joan of Arc. Her phone rang. It was Raja.

"Hey," she said, trying to sound like she couldn't care less if he ever called her again.

"Hey," he said, and then said what no girl ever wants to hear from a man she likes: "Look."

"I don't like 'look.'"

"I won't be able to make it tonight, after all," he said.

"Well, your *girlfriend* will be disappointed."

"Stop acting spoiled," Raja said, then told her he would see her in Paris in a week, just as they had planned, and "appropriately thank" her for her help, and her trust, these last weeks. What Nikki knew—or, what Nikki had been told and believed—was exactly what Raja told me he told Dasha. Raja had told Nikki we'd had an affair while I was married to Marcus, and that I had gotten pregnant, and that I had gone to the Cap to process it all. The loss, the baby. For Nikki, the story tracked perfectly, not only with what she observed but with her instinct. It tracked with her knowledge of who Raja was, and with what she had come to know of me. That's how to tell if a lie stands up to scrutiny, when it stress-tests well with a skeptic. And Nikki was skeptical about everything.

Nikki knew Raja had known her mother and stepfather "here and there" through the years, and that both Raja and her stepfather had worked for their respective governments, Edouard in Moscow in the military, and Raja in Lebanon in what Nikki had always believed was a role kind of like "financial attaché to the President." Even though there had always been rumors Raja was aligned with the Americans, later rumors about an alliance with Iran, *always* rumors about Israel. Nikki loved rumor. Nikki knew Raja was among the most attractive men she'd ever met, and she would fairly often fantasize that, one day, Raja would whisk her away to a life of "important things." Nikki craved depth but had no idea how to find it. On meeting Raja for the first time when she was barely thirteen, Nikki had, like me, noticed his bodyguards. And while a bodyguard might, to another kind of girl, indicate the threat of near violence, Nikki thought the bodyguards were cool. And yet, while Nikki grew up inside or, depending on

your definition, *adjacent* to the secret world, Nikki was ignorant
about how things worked. About danger. Dasha wasn't a woman
inclined to impart wisdom, but the one lesson, as she saw it, she
had worked hard to teach her daughter was the idea that their life,
while privileged, was true.

What Nikki did not know, and would only learn later, was
that her mother and stepfather's marriage had always been the
kind of lie that makes for a practical and, often, happy match.
Over a decade before I had arrived at the Cap, Edouard's boss had
told him he needed a wife, that it would "calm him down." Dasha
was right there in the office, and she knew all Edouard's secrets;
there was a level of mutual respect. Dasha was a widow, then, her
late husband had been killed in Ukraine and had been Edouard's
close friend. Dasha was all the things most men want in a wife,
beautiful, smart, amusing, and low-key. Dasha had also been a
fine mother to the daughter she had managed to raise on the margins of a career in Russian intelligence. Edouard, at the time, had
never been married. And he did want a child. And he had failed
to ever let himself fall in love. Love was an occupational hazard.
An hour after that chat with his boss, Edouard placed a brown
paper bag on Dasha's desk inside the safe house where they were
stationed in Beirut. Inside the bag was a three-carat Asscher-cut
diamond, "for ring or necklace," he had said. They spoke English
to each other at the time. Feeling magnanimous he had added,
"Your choice." Edouard's salary wasn't enough for that kind of
diamond, but Edouard had never been dependent on a salary.
Edouard's father, who had also worked for Mother Russia, had
been one of the original oligarchs. His death had left his son a
very rich man. Rich, and lost.

A week after Edouard placed that bag on her desk Dasha had
already organized the setting of the ring, complete with a tiny

bird engraved on the underside of the stone, invisible to anyone but known to her, a nod to the first Fabergé egg given by Czar Alexander III to the czarina. Dasha felt the bird would bring fertility, though she suspected if she had shared this with Edouard, he would have found it absurd, too romantic. She thought she knew Edouard and knew he was many things, but not romantic. She and Edouard were married on the beach at night, no witnesses, a young, local Russian orthodox priest officiating. It was less than two weeks later that a young woman walked into the lobby of the Hotel Albergo in Beirut, where Edouard was waiting to meet an asset. Something about her evoked a visceral reaction in him, entirely against his will. She wasn't like other girls he had been with. There was something so unpretentious about her, a level of vulnerability. She had a velvet ribbon in her hair. Edouard watched as she asked the concierge shyly for a matchbox she then used not to light a cigarette, but rather the tea candle on the table where she sat and started to read. On seeing all that, the ribbon and the candle and the book, Edouard's rough heart shattered into a thousand pieces. And Edouard gets what Edouard wants, so the asset would have to wait, and an hour later he and the young woman, who had told him her name was Sophie, lay in bed in the presidential suite. The idea he had broken a brand-new vow didn't bring Edouard shame. It brought relief. When you know the hurricane is coming you pray for it to come now, you want to be on the other side, God speed the plow.

"I could get pregnant," Sophie had said, according to Raja, who'd heard the tapes. Even then, Edouard's every move was tracked. CIA, Mossad, and MI6 knew not only where he dined and where he took long runs on Sundays, they knew how many lovers he had met since his arrival in Beirut. They knew that, in a classic lapse of tradecraft, Edouard took all his women to the same suite in the same hotel where he had made a deal with the hotel's manager. The deal was that in exchange for bringing him business the manager would keep the suite empty. Though what the manager *really* wanted was a house near the beach, which Israeli intelligence had provided, later, in exchange for the manager's compliance, and discretion. When Sophie told Edouard she might get pregnant Edouard told her that would make him happy, and he had meant it.

"I will call him Felix, after my father" was the last thing Sophie said, when it was all over and in the kind of moment where anything can be said safely, the moment when you think you will never see each other again. Edouard and Sophie were apart for two hours before meeting up again, and again the next night and the night after that and, within a week, Edouard had Sophie set up in a flat. Within a month it was all agreed. He would leave his new wife. They would start a family. They would live in Switzerland. Sophie didn't need a diamond, she just needed him. All he had told her was that he "worked in the Russian diplomatic corps." Sophie never saw the safe house. Sophie never saw a gun. Sophie never met Dasha, or Nikki.

All Nikki knew on the morning of Edouard's birthday was that she had a fierce crush on an older man her mother would deem entirely inappropriate, and that it was time for her to leave the Cap once and for all, grow up, evacuate the nest, find herself. Her plan, if you had asked her around noon on that day, in the hour at which she was more fully formulating it, was to return to Paris, complete her medical degree, and start a new life less defined by her family and their exotic temperaments. Nikki would miss Edouard. She admired him for what she experienced as a deft handling of power, she had recognized some of the visitors to the Cap and put at least a few of the pieces together, and she knew about Edouard's family. She also knew that to remain at the Cap was to retreat, not advance. She was too young to retire to beach life but also, arguably, too old to be considered "a girl" who might be taking a "break" before, for example, a new school year, a new career. Though that is exactly what it had been, at the start, when Dasha called Nikki and asked her daughter to come home and stay with them. Nikki had made up her mind to leave banking, and become an obstetrician. Medicine, then, seemed like hard work and delivered a level of depth. Delivering new life, how could that not bring meaning and joy. And, though it might not be lucrative, Nikki would never need money. It turns out money, not the ring, was what sealed the deal of Dasha's choice to marry Edouard. How Edouard had promised, then put carefully into writing, that Nikki would always be taken care of.

On the morning of his birthday, I like to think Edouard opened his eyes and looked at that photograph at the foot of his bed and felt a sense of peace. I like to think he was happily surprised by Felix and the cupcake and deeply proud of the family he had built, the young son he was raising with manners and empathy, this magical home he loved and might have lived in for many years, all the things he had accomplished. A long career "serving others," he could reasonably say, as if he'd been a missionary or a priest. By the morning of his birthday, Edouard had spent almost four decades participating, in various ways, in a war that was called "cold" before heating up again in places like Tripoli, Damascus, and Mogadishu. Places that served as appropriate proxies. Places that knew well destruction. Places like Beirut, where Edouard had been born to his "scholar" father and schoolteacher mother. His father had been posted in Lebanon as a young officer in the late 1950s and fallen in love with it. His father had been a loyal foot soldier to the Motherland and was rewarded for his loyalty.

A place can become part of an identity, and so later when
Edouard not only experienced his greatest tragedy, but also carried out his single most important operation in Beirut, it felt less
like a coincidence than like God's great plan. If you believe that
God takes and he gives, that is. The Beirut operation was deeply
personal, the worst kind. A personal operation requires emotional investment, and the high risk of a deeper, more philosophical sense of failure if things don't work out. You never want an
operation to be personal but so many are, ask Achilles. The Beirut
operation had been so personal in fact that Edouard's boss, at the
time, had signed off on it on the sole condition that Edouard find
someone else to pull the trigger.

"You're too close to it," was how his boss put it. His boss was
childless, so the "it" Edouard was close to, the "it" Edouard had
suffered, was foreign to him. Edouard's boss, like so many men
in that line of work, at that time, blinked at death. A real reckoning with loss simply isn't in the cards for them, maybe later upon
retirement, when you're holding a grandchild in your arms and
can look back not in anger but with dispassion, clarity, gentle
regret.

Emotion cannot factor into operations unless, of course,
love is involved. Or unless you were, like Edouard, a little different than most other operators. Edouard, since he was a boy, had
simply felt everything too deeply. He was probably meant for a
kinder, gentler line of work, as a professor or a painter. He had
decided to become a soldier believing it would please his father
but then had happened to excel at it, so much so that he would
become, by forty, one of the most decorated and in-demand killers of his generation, invited to shake the hands of Russian politi-
cians and aristocrats, his name spoken in hushed, rageful tones
by international leaders. Edouard had served in Russia's "white"

forces before transitioning to "intelligence" work and, eventually, blessed by a series of increasingly powerful admirers, crossing over into the private sector to mind a family office whose holding company's assets spanned six time zones and even more currencies. The lines separating public from private in Russia are not lines at all, they're small private pools, kept temperate and full. The oligarchs' relationship to Russia's various intelligence agencies is like the color blocks in a Rothko, a carefully calibrated blur. Edouard's life had been lived quietly but at the very apex of a certain kind of power. Rare air, indeed.

"Get someone young," his boss had said, as Edouard looked at a map of the city's streets, the route they would travel. What his boss meant was, *someone expendable, just in case.*

Edouard, yes, was by that time a little past the sell-by date for "front line" work. Most of his peers were either retired, rich and happy, or safely behind elegant desks in Moscow or Saint Petersburg. The idea was ever thus. Have the young Turks risk their lives. And yet, while he was no longer quite a wunderkind Edouard had amassed reputational power, which meant he could do what he wanted. An official order was, by that time in Edouard's life, simply a "suggestion." And he had made up his mind that *that* day and that operation would be his last. He would finish this one job, leave Lebanon, leave government, and retreat from the world. He would learn new things. He would process loss. And, above all, he had a baby boy to raise. Edouard wanted that boy to have a father who was present, who could teach him chess and how to swim a perfect butterfly stroke. A father to show the boy the world, to be there for every birthday, to answer the hard questions and, later, to pose them.

"Just don't fuck this one up," his boss called after him, as Edouard left the room, raising his middle finger behind his back.

And yet.

And yet I still like to think Edouard, on the morning of his birthday, left his bedroom, in his bathrobe, and spent time contemplating his paintings, even though the truth is that Edouard woke up that day, looked at the photograph at the end of his bed, and thought about Beirut. He had not fucked it up. Everything had gone exactly to plan. Not a single stone unturned. Beirut, for Edouard, had been an unmitigated success. And yet it hadn't brought him happiness. It hadn't brought him peace. Peace comes from other things.

*

Dasha did a beautiful job. The house had never looked more magical, hundreds of candles everywhere, peonies bursting from glass goblets lining all the paths and the outlines of the pergola. The guests who'd arrived that day didn't speak English. I had assumed they were family but couldn't be sure. Everyone seemed happy. I was seated at the opposite end of the table from Dasha and Edouard, next to Felix.

"I don't want you to go," Felix said, not looking at me. He'd barely touched his food. He was wearing a suit and tie, which made him look like he was auditioning for the role of an adult, which I found moving. He was growing up so fast.

"You can come visit."

"It's not the same," he said.

And I knew that was true.

I had told him, reluctantly, earlier, that I would be leaving in the morning. It was time. I knew I had to go back and, for one thing, see a doctor. I had to plan a life. I had to collect those pieces of me. I looked around the table that night and knew one thing very clearly, that this was not my family. I was the foreigner here. That these were not my friends. Dasha would be pleased to dispose of me and while Felix would miss me, he would forget, children have such short memories. Even then, if you had asked me about the color of my mother's hair when I was a child, before she had started dyeing it blond, I am not sure I could remember. Was it a little red? Or was it that flat, dirty brown. Raja had instructed me to "listen closely" during my days at the Cap, but what had I really learned. The helicopter, Raja had promised, would arrive at noon tomorrow. My plan had been to wake Felix early, take him for one last swim.

Dasha made a toast, then invited everyone down to the beach for the fireworks. As guests stood and started to gather along the path, I could see Edouard and Dasha arguing. I didn't want Felix to see, so I tried to distract him.

"And *when* you come visit, we can go to a football match," I said. "You can teach me how it all works."

"I would like that," he said.

The fight at the other end of the table was escalating, and Felix noticed.

"My father wants to go to bed. She never leaves him alone. She's never forgiven him."

"Forgiven him for what?"

And as Edouard walked off in the opposite direction, away from the beach, Dasha brushed past us without saying a word. Felix and I sat in silence. He tapped his fork on the edge of his glass, as if he planned to make a toast, too. We were still sitting there when I heard the fireworks start a few minutes later, heard the music rise. It was from the opening of the ballet *Swan Lake*, scene one. Looking up, I could see the explosions of color over the water and remembered the first time I had looked out over that ocean. The dream I had had of Marcus and me on the dock, the beast in the water. "Swans are incredibly violent," Edouard told me, when I had asked about his interest in the music on one of our walks. "*Swan Lake* is really a story about rage." I had said I did not see it that way, and he said, "One day you will."

Felix put his fork down.

"I need to tell you something," he said.

"You can say anything to me," I said.

"I think I love you."

*

And it was probably at the exact moment that the word "love" left Felix's mouth that Edouard entered the lemon grove. He was moving slowly. He was tired and, for the first time, felt old. Also, he'd been drinking, which he never did, perhaps in an effort to not think about Beirut, not think about his loveless marriage, not think about Sophie or about the son he adored who would never know the true love of a mother. As Edouard came through the grove it would certainly have surprised him to see a woman standing in the clearing, lit by the small white lights above the door to the museum. The woman was not one of the guests, which might have made Edouard wonder if he was seeing a ghost. And at that moment it occurred to Edouard that perhaps it had all been a dream, not only the compound at the Cap but also the Asscher-cut diamond placed on Dasha's desk, the killings in Beirut, and the baby placed in his arms in the operating room. All the wars that were really just one war, the targeting and developing of assets, the unending plays for power and redemption, self-loathing gradually obliterated by pride in the mission, good work, "the long game." If it had all been a dream, Edouard thought, standing there under the stars, it had been a wondrous one.

Edouard would not have tried to run, quite the contrary. Edouard would probably have walked right up to her, and she would have stood very still as he did. He would have been amused by her height, how she was as tall as he was. And as he got close, she had mouthed one word to him in Russian, and the fact that she knew his native language amused him. It would only be seconds later, when Edouard was a little farther into the clearing, the fireworks so loud it was as if they were exploding inside his brain, that Edouard could see clearly, thanks to the moonlight, that the woman held something in her hand. And even from ten yards away he immediately would have recognized the make and model of the weapon; he had carried the very same one, once. And looking at the woman he suddenly knew, instinctively, exactly why she was there, and also that she would not have come alone. You don't come alone to this kind of thing. It doesn't work like that. And so, as she raised her weapon, Edouard turned to see who was behind him.

In a Tokyo hotel room, Raja checked his watch.

It was the middle of the night.

Raja was thinking, he later told me, of a line from a T. S. Eliot poem he loved: *Hurry up please its time.*

And though the man Edouard expected to see when he turned was in fact there, just off to the left, and was also carrying a gun, Edouard didn't notice him at first. The first thing Edouard saw when he turned was his son, Felix, running as if he was moving on goal in any one of the hundred-plus games he'd played across the Cap's lawns these last months, running straight toward his father as if with an instinct to save him, as if Felix knew something the rest of us did not. If Felix was running to save someone that night, though, it was not his father. Felix was running to save himself, though he might not have put it as dramatically. Felix was running toward love, and away from pain. Felix knew the one person who loved him above all was his father, and he also knew that within hours, when I left, he would lose the first real friend he had ever made, the first person who he felt cared for him for who he was, not because of who his father was, who his grandfather once had been. The first person not to see the shame he felt about the loss of his mother even though that was not his fault. Felix, on that night, was finally over long dinners with strangers, over being nine and isolated and told what to do. Felix had, by that night, become bored of searching for seashells and *very* bored of Nikki's narcissism, to say nothing of how he felt about his stepmother. And for some reason, as the first fireworks popped over the ocean, and after he had said the word "love" for the first time to someone other than his father, Felix had had enough of it all, he simply wanted to be a boy and, in that moment, to cry to his father and to be held. You cannot really blame him, can you?

As the boy's increasing speed closed the gap between him and his father, Edouard could see me, too. I was only feet behind Felix. I had tried to stop him when he got up from the table, leaving his jacket on the back of the chair. When he had started walking toward the house. I thought he was angry at me. And I had my own instinct that something bad might be happening that night. Though no one had said the word, if I had cared to line up the fact pattern, the silk map, and the allusions to "Aleksey," the clues Jack dropped the day we met and the select parts of the mission he'd shared, I would have known my time there would not pass without tragedy. I had not lined up the fact pattern, though, people rarely do. I was entirely consumed with other things, with the life growing inside me, probably unconsciously with the death of my husband. I was not worried about Edouard, Edouard seemed impenetrable. And I was completely focused on Felix. I wanted to tell him that I loved him, too. I wanted to tell him that, if he wanted, he could come with me, tomorrow at noon, that I would take care of him. I felt with complete confidence that this was the right thing and that it would make everyone happy. Felix deserved a normal life. We all do.

I remember reaching out and how I could almost touch the tail of Felix's shirt, buoyed by the wind behind him, when the shots were fired. Four shots in all. Though if you had been there, you would have sworn you heard nothing but the pop of fireworks across the sky, the Tchaikovsky, the wind as it rose.

"What time will the fireworks start," Raja wanted to know, in the very last exchange we had had before he'd left for Japan.

"I don't know," I had said.

"Find out."

All I asked was for was a promise the helicopter would be on time, that then it would be over, that then I would be free.

"You're free now," he said. "You've always been free."

What I didn't know until later was that the fireworks had been a gift from Nikki, courtesy of Raja. Raja had even helped Nikki select the music when Dasha had asked if they could score the display to something Edouard loved. You see, Raja had learned years ago something even Dasha never knew, because all men hide their weaknesses, that Edouard didn't like loud noises. Edouard despised fireworks. And it had nothing to do with war. Edouard didn't like fireworks because they reminded him of Sophie. Raja knew all this from one of the hundreds of taped conversations he'd listened to so many times they were almost committed to memory. This particular conversation, recorded in the private dining room of a Viennese bank, included Edouard's casual reference to "a friend," though he did not say her name, only that because of her he hated fireworks. And so, on hearing about the fireworks for the first time with Dasha's toast, Edouard was angry. This is what he and Dasha had argued about, not at all fair to Dasha but emotions are rarely fair. Her choice of fireworks felt to Edouard like an attack, and at that moment their marriage, for him, felt one attack shy of collapse. Dasha felt she was simply holding up her end of the deal, that the Russians who were there that night would expect a certain extravagance, this was not a Black Sea beach, after all. Dasha wanted to show she was a woman of a certain standing, that she had taken care of her man, and that they had created a unique oasis safe from prying American eyes. And that, above all, Edouard was in his prime. Edouard was eligible. Edouard was *due*. Most Russians have a need to show, a quality that's been consistent since the revolution. Most Russians, but not Edouard. Edouard relied on discretion. And so while Dasha felt she was doing her job, Edouard felt she had launched a grenade. Dasha pleaded with him to relax, come to the beach, give it a try. She made clear she could not possibly cancel a fifty-thousand-euro explosives show. Edouard had said simply, fine, go ahead. Go ahead, but not with me. Edouard told Dasha he was going to bed.

*

Felix was only feet from his father when Felix dropped to the ground, as if he'd tripped. As I reached out to catch him, I looked up at Edouard, who was screaming, though no sound was coming out. Or was it that I could no longer hear, that I had gone deaf from the proximity of the shots. I remember feeling my right eardrum pop, like someone had run a knife across my collarbone. I was still moving but Felix was drifting away from me rather than coming closer. I was falling. And then everything went white. Bright, blistering white. A snowstorm of consciousness.

Hurry up please its time.

*

When I opened my eyes, Raja was sitting on the edge of the hospital bed, holding my hand.

"Felix," I said.

It felt like an elephant was sitting on my chest.

A sign on the wall was in French, so I knew I was still in France. If I closed my eyes, I could see Felix fall to the ground in front of me. I could see Edouard beyond him. And, pushing deeper into memory, I thought I could see a woman standing behind Edouard. I knew exactly who it was and why she was there. As I drifted in and out of consciousness Raja said, "I am so sorry," and it was then that I could see he was crying, and then that I felt tears start to form in the corners of my eyes.

He was sorry for my loss, another loss, the unimaginable loss no parent should ever have to bear.

I had lost the baby.

You can actually feel your heart break, even though it doesn't make a sound.

It wasn't Raja's fault, was it. Only one person had made the choices that led to that hospital bed, and she made them without ever being coerced or threatened.

"Felix," I said again, like Felix could save me, like I needed to know he was all right.

Raja squeezed my hand. I pulled it away and moved it over

my stomach, across my pelvis, gently tapping each hip bone, as if taking inventory of what remained. And it was as if for the first time and, at long last, my body started to process it all. Marcus was never coming back. There was truly nothing left of him. A nurse entered and said, "There is someone here who would like to see you." I turned toward the door and there he was, in his own little blue hospital gown, those enormous eyes and that wide smile. He walked over and, not acknowledging Raja, handed me a Coke.

"Hello, you," I said.

"Hello, you."

X

SUGAR CUBES

Dasha stayed at the Cap. Under new, more casual rule, the house changed. Rather than the chronic in- and outflow of business-men, or "associates," the compound would, in its later incarna-tion, only open to guests on occasion, and that usually meant Nikki's friends, an international set of young doctors and lawyers and bankers from Paris who would arrive with babies, later tod-dlers, eventually teenagers, in tow. They had no clue, or interest in, the house's past, though there were rumors about an accident that had taken place years ago. Nikki's friends and their children would have known nothing about the career, later death, or, it was sometimes rumored, *disappearance* of Nikki's stepfather. It was known that he had served in the Russian army. It was known that his marriage to Dasha wasn't really one of love. And the specula-tion had always been that, like many men before and after him, a night arrived when Edouard had simply had enough, and so had walked away from marriage, life, responsibility. This theory never quite made sense, though, as what man would leave not only a precious collection of paintings but a young son whom, by all accounts, he adored. To any parent, the willful abandonment of a child is unfathomable. "Unless you're in a war," one of Nikki's friends said once, and Nikki hadn't qualified that.

Nikki would casually assure her friends, if they asked, that Edouard had been a quiet man, a scholar, a lover of art, and that he had died of a heart attack in her mother's arms. She would tell you if you asked that Edouard had been a very caring husband. She would tell you his money, some of which had generously been placed into a trust for her benefit, derived from "a lucky accident in Azerbaijan." If anyone asked about a rumor that her father had served as an assassin for Russian intelligence, Nikki would tell you her little brother, who was by then living in London, "likes to romanticize." Which was true. Yet Felix would never have romanticized his father. Felix knew just enough of the truth, and that suited him.

Felix's memory of that night hinged on the moment he'd tripped while running toward his father. He had no memory of guns, of the woman who stood on the other side of his father or the man whose shot had grazed his shoulder. Felix did remember, and would hold close, the typed letter his father had left on his pillow and which Dasha had brought to the hospital. In it, Edouard had written of his great pride in Felix. Of his deep love for Felix's mother. And of how he, Edouard, knew that whatever happened in Felix's life he would always have the confidence of having been loved deeply. In the letter's last line Edouard explained that he had to go away for a while but that he would be back one day. Felix's belief that day would come gave him a clarity that things would ultimately end well, not unlike a Catholic's belief in heaven. That clarity of inevitable, happy conclusion would result in a very happy life for Felix as he grew up. As a young man he entered the world of professional sports, following his passion. And often when he watched a game, at first from the field as a young assistant coach, later as general manager, and, finally, as a chairman and owner, Felix would recall what Edouard used to say, that football is like life. "Men are born to be brutal," Edouard had told his son so many times. Sport, Edouard had said, provides "a safe place," a veneer of acceptability, for man's violent tastes. Sport, and war.

*

Nikki would often offer to walk visitors across the beach and up the stone steps I had once walked and loved. She would lead them across the outcropping's flat top and over to the small ledge and to the grave, the sight of which never failed to elicit a gasp. "This was Edouard's favorite spot," Nikki would say, when showing off that cross in the moonlight. She would tell you Edouard had bribed a priest in Rome to help him steal the cross from the apse in San Carlo alle Quattro Fontane. That Edouard identified with the church's architect, Borromini, and that he didn't consider the theft a crime against God, or against Borromini, but rather an acknowledgment of his admiration of what was, in his view, a divine, singular accomplishment. Nikki never told anyone Edouard hadn't been buried there, that for all she knew he hadn't been buried at all. Dasha privately maintained Edouard was alive and had selfishly orchestrated his exit from the Cap. In the end Nikki and Dasha and Felix would all hold on to separate fictions about the man who'd been so central to their lives. In the end, in a way, he'd lied to them all.

I knew Edouard was dead.

I knew exactly how he died, and why.

I knew there would never be any incentive for the truth to come out, no incentive for "the law to step in," for final confessions, no incentive to end the cycle of killing.

War endures by design. The history of war is a history of romance and mission, of malice slapping the wrist of good intent. The history of war is a history of action, reaction, repeat. War is tragedy, and tragedy, Aristotle knew, is a game of subtraction, a game of loss.

*

The further away I moved in time from my days at the Cap, the more I saw Edouard and Raja and Marcus as variations on a theme. How they each had done what they needed to do. If you asked me, later, about the father of my child, the child who had never had a chance, the child who had been conceived in the definition of *behind the eight ball*, I would tell you his name was Marcus. I would tell you Marcus had "died young, like most heroes," and that while I would have loved to bury him overlooking water, over the Bosporus or in the cliffs at Nazaré, in the end I buried his ashes according to a note in his will, in his hometown of Crozet, Virginia, on the grounds of Our Lady of the Angels Monastery. Marcus had quietly supported them for years. I made a habit of visiting each Christmas Day, and every year someone had always arrived before me, lain a wreath bursting with holly berries, a tiny American flag pressed into its leaves. I never saw him, but I knew it was Raja. Raja would have come in the early morning. He would have sat with his old friend as the sun came up and reminded Marcus how they had crossed that one-yard line, it was over, they could let go. And I always imagined that and thought at least one of them was at peace at last.

*

The paintings were eventually sold at auction. And one day, it won't surprise you to know, the one Edouard had said was his favorite arrived on my doorstep, and the card read, "He would have wanted you to have it." I hung it on the wall at the foot of my bed, and now it's the first thing I see in the morning and the last thing I see before I close my eyes at night. Sometimes when I close my eyes, I imagine I am in Jefferson's bed at Monticello, or the bed on the boat after my wedding as it sped toward Split. I imagine I am enclosed and taken care of, in a world of order.

*

I am not even forty, but I feel old.

And while I didn't alter my garden back to what it once was, I did make changes.

I brought back the roses.

I expanded the pond.

And, in the eastern corner, if you look closely underneath the rhododendron, you will notice two small stones. One is marked M, for Marcus. And one B, for Baby. I never named him in the end, though the French doctor confirmed it was a boy.

*

There is another boy who comes to my garden every day after school now. He likes to take his shoes off and walk across the shallow pool. He has a pet rabbit he often brings who likes sugar cubes. The boy lets the rabbit explore, knowing it will always return. And when the rabbit returns, the boy holds his little hand out patiently, then sometimes pulls it back when the rabbit gets close. A tease, a flirt, a hunter, all qualities I know are in his genes going back generations. He is a boy with deeply loving instincts. If you look closely, you will see his name embroidered on his favorite jumper, which he sometimes wears five days a week, it's his favorite, and one he will soon outgrow. He calls me *tía*, Spanish for "aunt," his mother is from Santander. When his mother met his father, Felix, at a football match in Madrid, Felix told her, "If we fall in love there is only one person in my life you need to know." I was the witness at their wedding in Granada.

Felix and I rarely talk about the Cap. If he had asked, I would have told him anything and everything, but he never asks. Once, his wife inquired about the small scar on his left shoulder. The bullet was not meant to harm Felix but rather to remove him from the narrative, to spare him from having to witness what came next. Jack called it "a mercy shot." Jack was trained to know how to aim to lightly wound. It was not the first, or last, shot Jack would have to take at a child.

"That's from when they removed his wings," I said, before Felix had a chance to answer.

His wife liked that line and, one summer on Patmos, I heard her repeat it to a table of friends.

After that she called Felix "my angel."

Occasionally, the story you need fits the fact pattern perfectly.

Felix would have told me anything, too. He would have kept my secrets. It would take time before Felix, as he neared thirty, would start to think about loss. That's what happens when you have a child, everything is suddenly, urgently fragile. Maybe when Felix looked at his son, all those years later, he would begin to question what it would feel like to have to say goodbye one day. Maybe he would, one day, question that letter left on his pillow at the Cap. How it was typed, not handwritten. Felix had never seen a typewriter in the compound. And Edouard, Felix knew, rarely wrote anything down. Yet that letter sat framed on Felix's desk in Chelsea. If anyone had cared to try to trace its origins, they might have discovered it was not typed at the Cap compound at all, but rather on a neighboring property, on an old Corona. When Annabel saw the typewriter, she had the idea for the letter, and called Raja so he could dictate. Raja didn't have a child, but he knew Felix, and he knew what Felix would need to hear.

Felix, like me, had been raised with secrets. Felix also had been raised with a chronic illness that required vigilance, humility, a certain letting go. Modern medicine would, eventually, bring relief but the threat of another "episode" was always there. That threat gave Felix a fierce gratitude that we should all have. His illness, undefinable in his childhood, had been narrowed down by modern doctors to a shock he had experienced in the womb. Felix always maintained his mother died as the result of a botched C-section, in a poor hospital. Felix never asked me about her, but when Edouard's bedroom at the Cap was finally emptied and the little museum razed, Russian intelligence burned it all except for the photograph of Sophie. That was sent to Felix, with compliments of the President himself.

*

In the weeks after my exit from the Cap, before Felix had moved away from Dasha to try to find his maternal grandparents in Switzerland, he called often. One night, he shared the fact that he'd been having a recurring nightmare, and it always started with a walk he had taken with Edouard early on the morning of Edouard's birthday, after Felix had brought that cupcake.

After the cupcake but before the green Citroën pulled into the gravel drive of the neighboring property and slid to a stop underneath the wide stone porte cochere. Well before Jack had run a bath, one of many pre-mission rituals, before Annabel had laid out a simple lunch of meats and cheese and walked Jack and Jill through final questions, choices, and contingencies. In fact, at the exact moment Edouard and Felix were crossing through the lemon grove on their way to the beach, Annabel was placing an encrypted call to Raja, who was, by that time, hard at work doing advance on a new project, in Tokyo. The fact that Raja had left France indicated either complete confidence in his team or, though less likely, fear of failure. Maybe Raja wanted to be as far away as possible from France that night. He had lit the match. He would be responsible. Raja knew if things had not gone well his government, and other "stakeholders" in the operation, would abandon him. Annabel told Raja it was wise for him not to be there, that her work was easier "without you editing every line." Annabel assured Raja there would be no need for editing that night. She planned to leave the following morning for Munich. Her next job promised to be far more complex.

Spies, like sharks, die if they stop moving.

The real reason Raja had removed himself, though, was one not even Annabel could divine. The real reason was emotion. He cared too much. The stakes were too high. And I was involved, an innocent civilian, the pregnant widow of a man he had once called his best friend. If something had happened to me, Raja would never have been able to forgive himself.

Felix described how, in the nightmare, Edouard had been in no rush at all. Edouard had sat with Felix and admired the paintings. As Felix ate the cupcake Edouard claimed he didn't want, Edouard told Felix the story of the Trojan War. He pointed out figures in the paintings that looked like flowers, or scribbles, and told his son how, if he looked carefully, he would see they were people. He told Felix about Achilles and Patroclus, Priam and Hector. He said the *Iliad* was "the greatest story ever told, because it has it *all*." "All" being glory and loss, the wrath of gods and the rage of men, love. He told Felix what *he* had learned from the story was that peace comes through a recognition of grace in all men. "Even in your *enemy*," Edouard said, and then Edouard's eyes had gone completely white, as if Edouard were no longer real. And that is where the nightmare always ended, with the white of Edouard's eyes. And so I asked Felix to tell me what had actually happened that morning.

That morning Edouard didn't talk about the *Iliad* at all. They had not looked at the paintings and Felix had not eaten the cupcake. What had actually happened was Edouard walked Felix to the beach where he told a story about a famous Italian architect, Borromini. Edouard described Borromini's churches and assured Felix that one day he would see them, too. He told Felix the one not to be missed was called San Carlo alle Quattro Fontane, "four fountains." And then Edouard had led Felix up the rocky stairs that he and I had walked so many times. When Felix saw the cross, he asked his father who was buried there. And before I could tell Felix I knew the answer he surprised me. "And then my father said the strangest thing," Felix said. I remember where I was when Felix said it. I was sitting on the floor of my new home in London, waiting for furniture to arrive. Edouard said, Felix told me, "It's not a burial, it's a monument."

And then Edouard removed the cross from its mossy base, "which wasn't easy," and laid it flat on the ledge. He showed Felix how on one side, the side facing back toward the compound, he had carved a tiny, almost imperceptible E into the stone, for

Edouard. And then he had turned the cross over and shown Felix the other side, the side that would face the ocean, "and so have the superior view." There Edouard had carved another letter: T. He told Felix *this* letter was for a man called Tracy, "the man I might have been." And then Edouard placed the cross back firmly in its base, kissed his young son, and told him he loved him.

"Why do you think he wanted to show me that," Felix asked.

Out my window I could see leaves changing color, it was autumn.

"Because he trusts you."

Nothing matters more than trust.

"Because he loves you," I added.

I was not ready to release use of the present tense when it came to Edouard.

Some things take time.

"I feel old," said Felix, before we hung up, which made me laugh.

"You are very, very, *very* old," I said.

*

There is an adage attributed to Albert Einstein. Einstein said that while he could not predict which weapons would be used to fight a third world war, a *fourth* world war would be fought "with sticks and stones." This has been interpreted to mean that the third world war will be so devastating there will be nothing left. The world will be reduced to rubble, sticks, and stones. I interpret it differently. The reason a fourth world war will be fought with sticks and stones is because sticks and stones will be, one day, the last step left in the evolution of war and espionage. Once war and espionage lap the limits of technological advancement, speaking of last acts, war will revert, become radically primitive. In that new world, the introduction of fire will once again count as revelation and symbol, the math of attrition will be calculated on a cave wall. In a world where any other form of communication is necessarily "insecure," the revolution will not be televised, the revolution will start with a silent hand signal in the forest.

It's been eighteen years since I left the Cap. The world has not changed that much even though I have. Things I once found foreign, or unacceptable, are just how it is. Truth is a toy I play with, like a toddler with jacks. I practice a level of mistrust with every story I hear, every product I am sold, every war I have been assured is "good," a "necessary intervention." And while I don't believe in the casual presence of assassins on every street corner, I no longer believe it is safe to sleep without a gun. I am an American asset based in the UK, after all. Once you've been the star of the third act, you cannot unsee what you have seen.

*

A garden has no age.

A garden has no allegiances.

A garden does not discriminate between an assassin and an angel.

A garden cannot lie.

If you come to my garden, and if you are patient, that rabbit will eventually appear.

If you are patient, you will see the little boy open his palm to reveal a pair of sugar cubes.

His world is not defined by anything other than the moment.

. . .

I am holding his jumper on my lap.
    His father, Felix, had the very same one when he was a boy.
    His grandfather, Edouard, had one, too.

I trace the lines of the needlepoint letters of his name with my
ring finger.
    I sewed them on myself.

    T
    R
    A
    C
    Y

This garden will be yours one day, Tracy.
And then you can make it entirely your own.
You can save us, Tracy. You can set us free. I believe that.

XI

BEIRUT

The Lebanese sky does not disappoint. As he drove his old Defender past the French ambassador's residence, I imagine Tracy Barnes was reminded of what Marcus would say whenever he saw something outrageously beautiful, the Sistine Chapel or Versailles, Masaccio's *Expulsion from the Garden of Eden* or Hadrian's Villa. He would say it to indicate how far he felt we'd fallen from a certain grace. He would say, "We live like pigs." And, in more ways than one, Barnes did live a little like a pig, at least in those days. Tracy had fallen in love with Beirut and planned to live there forever, or for as long as the U.S. government would allow him to stay. The posting had been his first choice. He was doing work he loved. His colleagues were brothers, he would risk his life for them, and had on more than one occasion. And though his generation of men and women had amassed a certain level of experience by that time in their lives, they still felt young, none were yet married, none were yet parents, all believed in what was still occasionally called "the mission," when it wasn't being called "the forever war." If America carried a spear in the new and uncertain century, Barnes and his team represented its tip. Bond was a lie, and Bourne was a lie, but the cowboys of American intelligence very much existed and had been, for a time, thriving. There, wherever "there" was, always far from home, they were kings. Identityless, homeless, probably poorer than you, they did not care. They were kings in the most powerful court in the world, the world of international espionage. And Tracy Barnes was thinking about kings that Lebanese morning as the sun came up, about Richard the Lionheart in particular, whose biography he had been reading on the recommendation of an old friend, Taran Davies. Tracy was thinking about King Richard's marriage, in fact, at the exact moment that the bullet split the windscreen and entered his left eye, a shot with a precision he would have admired and envied, had he not been its target. And though in those seconds which felt like hours he imagined reaching for his pistol, and firing back, Tracy was a celebrated shot, the truth is that before his brain could send a signal to his hand, the second bullet hit. The windscreen shattered. The Defender spun once before flipping on its side in the wake of meeting up with a telephone pole, then came to a stop at the center of the intersection of one of the city's poshest districts.

If you had asked him later, if there had been a later, Tracy would have told you the Agency reports officer could claim with "high confidence" that he knew the identity of the man who had fired those shots, and why. Actions have consequences, especially in wars, and Tracy knew that he had been marked for dead the day he had attempted, and failed, to kill Aleksey Zhukov. He had made the mistake of taking *his* shot when he had it, of course he did, you follow orders in this line of work. You follow orders and you don't waste time, carpe diem, and all that. The only thing that trumps the perfect execution, and timing, of an order is bad luck. And, at the exact moment Tracy took his shot, Zhukov's very pregnant girlfriend was sitting beside him. And Zhukov had been hit but no one had tracked the fact that he had started wearing a vest, and so that shot wasn't fatal. Tracy later learned, though, that the stress of the attempt had sent the girlfriend into labor at thirty-three weeks. And while Langley knew the girl was "only" Zhukov's mistress, they had recently speculated that he planned to leave his wife, with whom he had no children, only a step-daughter, for this new girl once their baby boy was born, chatter having revealed the child's gender. What they did *not* know about the girlfriend was that she had an underlying heart condition. What they never could have predicted was that when she was lying on the operating table undergoing an emergency cesarean, that condition would trigger a heart attack and kill her. Her death the result of that ever-elusive element in espionage, the unknown unknown, the one outcome beyond all imagining, the only out-come that slips chatter's grasp and cannot be captured by a drone. The doctor had placed the tiny baby in his father's strong Russian arms and said, simply, "I am so sorry." The Russian could see that the baby had his eyes and hoped he would also have his mother's heart.

And when Aleksey, who went by many names throughout the course of his career to include, in the end, Edouard, a nod to his grandfather, Edvard, looked at the doctor and said, "Oh, *many* people will be sorry," he meant not only Tracy Barnes, who he knew with more than high confidence he would find one day, but also America. America the dreamer, the optimist, apotheosis of all things possible. America the proud and reckless. America, ultimately, the vulnerable. This was the America running through the Russian's mind as he rocked his baby to sleep that night, clear in the presence of a new patience he would be capable of now. America, the one country Aleksey would spend the rest of his life blaming not only for this loss, but for many, many others. If only

Aleksey and Tracy had had the chance to sit, maybe in some tent late at night when the rest of the world was sleeping and enough blood had been shed on all sides—if they had been able to sit, and talk, like Priam and Achilles, they might have discovered the things they shared, like loss. They might have wept and seen at once the joy and the futility in their work, seen that the reckoning they sought was the real chimera. And with this knowledge they might have made decisions so that their guests could sleep well. And, in doing that, they then might have found a will, and a way, while they were still young, to end the slaughter of their war, the true forever war, the last great game.

Tell me about a complicated man.
Muse, tell me how he wandered, and was lost
when he had wrecked the holy town of Troy,
and where he went, and who he met, the pain
he suffered in the storms at sea, and how
he worked to save his life and bring his men
back home. He failed to keep them safe; poor fools,
they ate the Sun God's cattle, and the god
kept them from home. Now goddess, child of Zeus,
tell the old story for our modern times.
Find the beginning.

—HOMER, *The Odyssey*,
THE EMILY WILSON TRANSLATION

Author's Note

In 1985 William Buckley, CIA Chief of Station in Beirut, was kidnapped and assassinated. Twenty-three years later, Hezbollah leader Imad Mughniyeh was killed in a car bombing in Damascus. That bombing was eventually revealed to have been a CIA/Israeli Mossad operation, presumed revenge for Buckley's death.

In *Ilium*, I tried to say something about war's essential subjectivity, how a hero to one side is an assassin to another. I tried to bring the reader inside the minds of the players on all sides of a brutal, violent, very high stakes game. And, especially, inside the mind of one woman who becomes involved not for love of her country but, simply, for love.

I have thought often about the small circle of people involved in any highly classified operation and eventually developed the idea of a story about a pair of interlocked killings, not unlike those of Buckley and Mughniyeh, operations separated by several years, or even a generation. Revenge, in a forever war, can take its time.

Acknowledgments

I could not have written this book without the belief, patience, and insights of Shelley Wanger and Eric Simonoff; Nicholas Latimer, Lisa Kwan, and Andrew Dorko; Sylvie Rabineau, Paul Haas, and Paul Bogaards. And, of course, Elliot Ackerman.

A NOTE ABOUT THE AUTHOR

Lea Carpenter is the author of two novels, *Eleven Days* and *red white blue*. She lives in New York.

A NOTE ON THE TYPE

This book was set in Adobe Garamond. Designed for the
Adobe Corporation by Robert Slimbach, the fonts are based
on types first cut by Claude Garamond (ca. 1480–1561). Garamond was a pupil of Geoffroy Tory and is believed to have followed the Venetian models, although he introduced a number
of important differences, and it is to him that we owe the letter
we now know as "old style." He gave to his letters a certain
elegance and feeling of movement that won their creator an
immediate reputation and the patronage of Francis I of France.

Composed by Westchester Publishing Service,
Danbury, Connecticut

Printed and bound by Berryville Graphics,
Berryville, Virginia

Designed by Soonyoung Kwon